Gunpowder and Tea Cakes

My Journey with Felicity

by Kathleen Ernst

American Girl®

Published by American Girl Publishing

17 18 19 20 21 22 23 LEO 10 9 8 7 6 5 4 3 2 1

This book is a work of fiction. Any similarity to real persons, living or dead, is coincidental and not intended by American Girl. References to real events, people, or places are used fictitiously. Other names, characters, places, and incidents are the products of imagination.

Cover image by Michael Dwornik and Juliana Kolesova

Cataloging-in-Publication Data available from the Library of Congress

For my family, with happy memories
of our visits to Colonial Williamsburg

BeForever™

The adventurous characters you'll meet in
the BeForever books will spark your curiosity
about the past, inspire you to find your voice
in the present, and excite you about your future.
You'll make friends with these girls as you share
their fun and their challenges. Like you, they are
bright and brave, imaginative and energetic,
creative and kind. Just as you are, they are
discovering what really matters: Helping others.
Being a true friend. Protecting the earth.
Standing up for what's right. Read their stories,
explore their worlds, join their adventures.
Your friendship with them will BeForever.

A Journey Begins

This book is about Felicity, but it's also about a girl like you who travels back in time to Felicity's world of 1774, just before the American Revolution. You, the reader, get to decide what happens in the story. The choices you make will lead to different journeys and new discoveries.

When you reach a page in this book that asks you to make a decision, choose carefully. The decisions you make will lead to different endings. (Hint: Use a pencil to check off your choices. That way, you'll never read the same story twice.)

Want to try another ending? Read the book again—and then again. Find out what happens to you and Felicity when you make different choices.

Before your journey ends, take a peek into the past, on page 176, to discover more about Felicity's time.

1

*B**rriiing!* When the last bell of the day rings, everyone in my class starts shoving stuff into their backpacks. It's springtime, and nobody wants to hang around school.

"Don't forget your assignment!" Ms. Deming calls. "Your persuasive essays about citizenship are due on Monday."

Right. We're supposed to explain the important role that everyday people play in government. Pretty boring. I haven't started writing. I know what I'll be doing all weekend, I think gloomily.

My friends Lauren and Amara are waiting in the hall. "Have you started your essays yet?" I ask.

"Mine's almost done," Amara says.

"Show-off!" Lauren teases.

Amara shrugs. "My parents won't let me participate in extra activities if I don't get my homework done. My African dance group is performing tomorrow night, and I have a rehearsal this evening." Amara loves to dance. Her mother was born in Senegal—a country in western Africa—and they both belong to the African dance group. Amara also takes ballet.

2

"Well, I haven't even started my essay," Lauren says as we walk outside.

"Me either," I admit.

"I've got more important things to think about today anyway," Lauren says. Her eyes are sparkling.

"What's going on?" I ask suspiciously.

"My mom is taking me to the animal shelter to pick out a puppy this afternoon!" Lauren exclaims.

"A puppy?" Amara squeals.

"Why didn't you tell us?" I demand.

"Because I wanted to surprise you!" Lauren says happily. "My mom said you both can walk to my house with me and come to the shelter with us. After we choose a puppy, Mom will drive you home."

Amara whips out her cell phone. "I'll let my parents know. My rehearsal isn't until eight o'clock."

Lauren turns to me. "You'll come too, won't you?"

I can tell she really wants me to come. And since I love animals more than just about anything in the whole world, I really want to go.

"I'm sorry, Lauren," I say quietly. "I can't—I have to go home."

"Do you need to call your dad?" Amara asks.

"You can borrow my phone."

"It's not that," I say. "I'm not allowed to go anywhere after school unless I clear it with my dad in advance."

"My mom will drive you home," Lauren says again. She looks confused. She can pretty much do anything she wants.

"My dad hasn't met your mom," I say miserably.

Amara is still holding out her cell phone. "Can your grandmother give you permission?"

Dad and I moved in with Grandma after my mom died last year. "No," I say, staring at the sidewalk. "I'm really sorry, but that's my dad's rule."

Turn to page 4.

4

For a long moment nobody knows what to say. Kids are shoving and shouting all around us, either heading home or lining up to get on a bus. My face feels hot.

"Your dad is really strict," Lauren finally says. "Well, I guess we'll see you later."

"Sure," I say. I hate disappointing my friends.

Lauren and Amara walk away. I turn toward home, with nothing to look forward to but cleaning in my grandmother's antiques shop and homework.

My grandmother's shop is in a really old brick building in Williamsburg, Virginia. My grandfather, who died before I was born, worked in a grocery store. My dad was an only child, and after he started school, Grandma kept herself busy during the day by buying and selling antiques. Her shop isn't crammed with all kinds of stuff like some antiques stores are. Everything is tidy, and she doesn't sell anything that isn't at least a hundred years old. Some of her things are more than two hundred years old.

When I open the door, there are no customers inside. "Hi, Grandma," I call.

To my surprise, Grandma and my dad come out of

the back office. Dad runs his own plumbing business, and he's hardly ever home so early.

He smiles. "Hey, how's your day been?"

Everything comes pouring out. "Dad, Lauren is picking out a new puppy this afternoon, and she invited Amara and me to go! Can I? Please? Maybe we could meet them at the animal shelter."

"I'm sorry," he says, "but I just stopped home for a minute. I have an emergency call. An elderly woman has a burst pipe and water all over her kitchen."

"You could just drop me off, and Lauren's mother will drive me home. Please?"

Dad just shakes his head. "I haven't met Lauren's mother yet. I'm sure you'll have plenty of chances to see the puppy."

But I want to help choose the puppy, I mutter in my head. I can't have a dog because the apartment we share with Grandma above the shop is small. We have a sweet yellow cat named Muffy, but Grandma thinks a dog would be too much trouble.

Dad starts to walk away, then turns back. "Cheer up, Pumpkin."

I sigh. Dad has called me that since I was a little

kid. Today it makes me feel like he thinks I'm still a little kid.

"We have a fun day planned for tomorrow, remember?" Dad is saying. "A daddy-daughter day at Colonial Williamsburg."

Colonial Williamsburg is a big historic park very close to where we live. People called interpreters work there. They dress up in old-time costumes to tell the story of the American Revolution, when the thirteen colonies broke free of British rule to become the United States of America. Sometimes they give tours of the old buildings. Sometimes the staff and volunteers at Colonial Williamsburg stage little plays right in the streets, and visitors can pretend they're townspeople.

My dad is a volunteer interpreter there, playing the role of a Patriot who wants independence. I've been accepted as a junior interpreter for the summer. I'll probably learn how to churn butter and bake bread, stuff like that. I agreed to do it because Dad wanted me to, but honestly, it's not how I would choose to spend my summer vacation. I'm a little worried that I won't know what to talk to visitors about. And going

to Colonial Williamsburg doesn't take the place of choosing a puppy.

"Don't wait dinner on me," Dad tells Grandma. Then he walks out the door.

"It's not fair," I mumble. "He's the strictest dad on the planet. Last week I asked if I could take horseback riding lessons, and he said I had to be sixteen years old before I could."

"Your dad was afraid you might get hurt if you take riding lessons," Grandma says. "And his rule about always knowing who you're with is just to keep you safe."

As if going to an animal shelter is dangerous! "It's like he doesn't trust me. He says I'm too young to babysit, even during the day."

"Oh, sweetie." Grandma looks sad.

"Can't you talk to him?" I plead. "I'm not a little kid anymore!"

Grandma shakes her head. "He's the parent. I can't second-guess his decisions."

So, I think, *I'm out of luck.*

Grandma changes the subject. "How was school today?"

I shrug. "School was okay. I have a lot of homework."

"I have some homework too," she says. "I purchased a treasure this afternoon, and I want to learn more about it. Want to see?"

She leads me to one of the glass display cases. Inside is a teensy-tiny portrait of a woman, strung on a fine chain like a necklace. Only the woman's head and shoulders show, but it's hard to see the details. Honestly, I don't know why an artist would go to so much trouble.

"What good was such a little portrait?" I ask.

"This miniature was painted in 1775—right around the time of the American Revolution," Grandma says. "Imagine what life was like before photographs and videos. If people were going to be separated for some reason, these tiny portraits helped keep memories close."

Grandma didn't say that the miniature might have been painted because the lady was so sick her family thought she might die, but I wonder if that was the reason. After my mom died it would have been nice to have a portrait of her, looking the way I want to remember her. Dad and I stopped taking pictures of

Mom after she got really, really sick. And the night she died Dad put away every framed photograph of Mom we had. I guess it hurt him to see her looking all happy and healthy, but I wish he hadn't done it.

Grandma closed the case so the portrait couldn't get dusty. "Well," she says, "shall we go upstairs and cook dinner? We're having spaghetti."

"Is it okay if I don't come up for a little while?" I ask. I take a special cleaning cloth from the stack under the counter, pretending I'm going to do chores. The truth is that between thinking about puppies and thinking about Mom, I'm half mad and half sad. I really need some time by myself.

"Of course," Grandma says. "I'll call you when dinner's ready." She locks the front door, puts the "Closed" sign in the window, and goes upstairs.

At least Grandma trusts me to dust her antiques, I think. *Even if Dad doesn't trust me to do anything.*

I give the case holding Grandma's new miniature a swipe. Then I open the door and lean closer, studying the lady. She's very pretty. And even though her hairstyle and clothes are old-fashioned, there's something about her expression that reminds me of Mom.

My throat closes up like it does whenever I think of my mother, and I get this tight feeling inside. Suddenly I miss Mom so much it's hard to breathe.

Before Mom died, I knew I was going to miss her. But I didn't realize how much was going to die with her. Mom was giving me guitar lessons, but now my guitar is hidden under the bed. Mom and I used to bake butterscotch brownies a lot, because my dad loved them, but I can't make them anymore because it makes him sad.

And Mom was the one who really encouraged me when I told my parents I want to be a veterinarian one day. She said she knew I could learn everything I need to learn if I set my mind to it. Dad doesn't discourage me, but he's a lot more interested in history, like Grandma.

Dad hardly ever mentions Mom, so I don't either. But everything would be different if she were still alive. I never felt as if I were being treated like a baby when Mom was around.

Gently, very gently, I pick up the tiny painting. The woman in the miniature portrait looks kind and understanding. It seems as if she's staring right into my eyes.

But something's wrong. The painted colors blur. I start to feel dizzy, so I squinch my eyes closed. The floor tilts beneath my feet. Everything whirls around. I know I mustn't drop the miniature, so I clench it in my hand. I'm really confused—and scared, too. What is going on?

Turn to page 12.

12

Before I can open my eyes, I hear shouting. It comes from a distance at first, but grows louder. The whirling feeling fades. The noise keeps getting louder, though. I open my eyes . . . and I have to fight away dizziness again, because I am not in my grandma's antiques shop!

Somehow I ended up outside, huddled behind a thick green hedge. All the commotion is coming from the other side of the hedge. Feet pound as if somebody is running. Men and women are yelling, and . . . is that hoofbeats? I have to see what's happening!

I spot an opening in the hedge, but when I start to hurry through, I trip and fall. I land hard on a walkway of crushed oyster shells. "Ow!"

"Have a care!" someone says. "'Tis a poor day to stumble, in this crowd."

It's a girl about my own age. Instead of shorts or jeans, she's wearing a long purple-striped gown—the kind of dress interpreters wear at Colonial Williamsburg.

"Are you a volunteer?" I blurt.

"That fall must have addled you," the girl says. "Only boys may volunteer."

She gives me a hand up, and I stagger to my feet. I finally get a good look around . . . and can hardly believe my eyes.

Am I dreaming? I wonder. *Did I sleepwalk?* I've never walked in my sleep before. But somehow I've ended up in Colonial Williamsburg. The big, beautiful brick building up ahead is the Governor's Palace. My dad has brought me here many times, but it's a very long walk from our house.

Interpreters are all around me, mostly hurrying in the same direction. And when I glance down, I discover I'm wearing the same kind of long dress the girl is wearing. Mine is cream-colored with little blue flowers. It's pretty, but it feels too tight. A white kerchief is tucked around my neck.

"Are you hurt?" the girl asks kindly. "My name is Felicity Merriman. What's yours?"

I tell her my name. "I—I don't think I'm hurt. But I'm confused! What is happening?"

"Have you just arrived in the city?" Felicity asks.

She must be one of the junior interpreters. She's really good, just like an actor. I decide to play along so I can sort out this mess. "It seems so."

Felicity doesn't look at all surprised. "Many have arrived since the royal governor schemed to steal the colonists' gunpowder from the Magazine in the dark of night."

My dad has explained that in colonial times, a Magazine was a place where people stored gunpowder, bullets, and other ammunition and weapons.

"Riders immediately carried the news all over the countryside," Felicity continues. "Patriots have been streaming into Williamsburg like a river in flood!"

I must be in the middle of a special event, I think. This one is really authentic. Men and women are gathering on the huge green lawn in front of the Governor's Palace. Some look curious, as if they don't know what's going on either. Some look really angry. The angry ones shout things like "Return our powder!" and "Storm the Palace!"

Two barefoot little boys wearing ragged clothes run past. They're no more than five or six, but I don't see any adult keeping an eye on them. A man waves a knife that looks really sharp. A woman limps by, and I can see she has a bad scrape on one ankle. A carriage passes, jolting terribly because of deep ruts in the dirt road.

But . . . that can't be. Dad and I have walked this road. It's paved.

My mouth goes dry. Something is truly and terribly wrong. It's not just that I somehow ended up in Colonial Williamsburg wearing a costume—it's that there are no modern visitors anywhere. Everything and everyone looks and sounds and feels real.

Too real. I've got to get out of here! But how?

Felicity turns away to watch a group of boys and young men playing drums and fifes march toward the Palace.

This all started when I picked up the miniature portrait of the pretty woman. I'd forgotten all about it, but I'm still clutching it in my left hand. I dart back through the gap in the hedge. Slowly I uncurl my fingers and stare into the painted eyes.

Turn to page 16.

16

The dizziness doesn't come as quite such a surprise this time. I close my eyes eagerly, hoping like crazy that this will work. And it does! The angry shouts fade away.

I wait until everything is silent before opening my eyes. And here I am, right back in Grandma's shop. I'm so relieved I almost collapse on the floor. It's me, in my own clothes, right where I belong.

But—how long was I gone? Grandma must have been worried! She keeps a pretty close eye on me when Dad's not around.

I carefully replace the miniature portrait. Then I race up the stairs to our apartment.

"I'm here, Grandma!" I cry, bursting into the kitchen.

She's just reaching for her apron, and turns with a surprised look. "Well, you changed your mind in a flash! I thought you wanted to stay downstairs for a moment or two."

I'm confused all over again. I must have been with Felicity for at least five or ten minutes, but it seems that here, no time passed.

"Well—um—I did," I stammer. "I mean, I do. I just

wanted to make sure you were all right."

"I'm fine, sweetie!" Grandma smiles as she ties the apron strings. "You run along."

Slowly I go back downstairs, back to the glass case. I'm afraid to even look at the portrait. Instead I think about Felicity. She seemed awfully nice. She was all alone, but she still took time to make sure that I, a stranger, was okay in the middle of all the uproar.

Now I'm worried about her.

I could go back, I think. *Just to make sure that Felicity is all right.*

I wouldn't be so scared and confused this time. Since I didn't get to go help pick out Lauren's puppy, I think I deserve an adventure. Best of all, I don't have to ask for permission! Dad will never know I'm gone.

I pick up the portrait again. This time I slip the chain over my neck. I take a deep breath. Then I turn the miniature so I can stare into the lady's eyes.

Noise fills my ears. I open my eyes and find myself right back behind the hedge in Colonial Williamsburg. This time I lift my long skirt and step onto the walkway without stumbling.

"There you are!" Felicity looks relieved. "When

I turned and found you gone, I was worried."

"I'm sorry," I tell her. "I—I, um, lost something."

"Did you find it?"

I feel for the miniature portrait. It's still hanging safely from its chain around my neck. "Yes," I say. I slip the necklace underneath the kerchief tied at my throat to keep it extra safe and hidden.

"Are you traveling alone?" Felicity asks. "You seem a stranger here."

"I do know Colonial Williamsburg a little," I tell her.

She looks startled. "Colonial Williamsburg? That's a strange way to refer to the town."

Of course! I think. *Everything is colonial in Felicity's time.*

I figure the best plan is to keep my story as close to the truth as possible. "How silly of me," I say. "Anyway, my father has brought me here several times. But . . . I don't know where he is right now."

"I'm not surprised you got separated in this excitement," Felicity says. "Would you like me to keep you company?"

"Yes, please," I say gratefully. If I'm going to wander around, I need a guide.

A boy's voice cuts through the clamor. "Felicity!"

Felicity whirls, then grins. "Ben! What are you doing?"

"Running an errand for your father," Ben says. He looks a few years older than Felicity and me. His brown hair is tied back in a ponytail. He wears pants that stop just below the knee, a shirt and vest, and a lacy white thing around his neck.

Ben seems kind of quiet. But when he looks at me, he removes his tricorn hat and actually makes a tiny bow—right there on the street! "I don't believe I've made your acquaintance."

Felicity introduces me and explains, "Ben lives with my family. He's apprenticed to my father, who owns Merriman's Store."

"But what are you girls doing here?" Ben asks. "I thought you were going to your friend Elizabeth's house, Felicity."

"I did go," Felicity says, "but no one answered my knock." She turns to me and adds in a low tone, "Elizabeth's parents are Loyalists."

"They best stay hidden for now," Ben says. "Patriot tempers are high after the theft of our gunpowder."

I notice he says "our" gunpowder. Ben must be a Patriot. I think of my dad, always studying so he'll do a good job playing the part of a Patriot at Colonial Williamsburg. I wish Dad could meet Ben!

"It may not be proper for you girls to stay out either," Ben is saying. "A mob is forming."

"But I want to see what happens!" Felicity protests. "People say several independent companies of militia are marching to Williamsburg!"

Militia? That means soldiers are on the way! My heart skips a beat. Do I want to stick around for that?

"'Tis exciting, to be sure," Ben murmurs. "I do believe 1775 might see the colonists' rebellion spread!"

I've traveled back to 1775, I think. It's unbelievable . . . but then I take another hard look around. I see a pig rooting in a pile of trash, and dust rising in the street where asphalt is supposed to be, and no sign of any modern people. And I do believe it.

"I do so wish to see the militia arrive," Felicity is pleading to Ben. "It will be exciting!"

"Indeed," Ben agrees. "But perhaps your new friend doesn't share that wish." He glances meaningfully at my dress.

I realize the skirt is dirty from my fall. There's even a tear where the fabric must have gotten caught on a twig. Ben must think I'm embarrassed to be seen like this.

"Oh, forgive me." Felicity grabs my hand as if we were old friends. "If we go home, my mother will find you some refreshment, and we can mend your gown. But if you wish to stay and see the militia arrive . . ."

I can tell that Felicity really wants to see if the angry crowd and militia can force the governor to return the gunpowder he stole. But I can only imagine what my dad would say if he knew I was in the middle of a crowd of armed people—with soldiers on the way! And honestly, it might be just as interesting—and safer—to go to Felicity's house.

To leave the crowd and go home with Felicity, turn to page 29.

To wait for the militia to arrive, turn to page 32.

"I think we should stay," I tell her. We're already right in the middle of something *huge*! Besides, messing around with gunpowder doesn't sound like a very good idea.

Felicity turns to Ben and his friend. "Godspeed your work!" Ben nods, and the boys slip away.

The soldiers' leader is bellowing for attention. "I am Captain Brandon!" His black tricorn hat is battered, and his boots are scuffed, but a bright red sash makes him look important. "As most of you know, the governor sent marines to steal our gunpowder in the dark of night. Well, we want it back!"

A lot of people cheer, but a few mutter and shake their heads. "That gunpowder belongs to the royal government!" somebody yells. "The governor has every right to it."

Felicity and I exchange wide-eyed glances. That Loyalist is brave to speak his mind in this angry crowd.

"If the governor had every right to the gunpowder, why did his men act in the dark of night?" Captain Brandon demands.

People around us mutter with agreement. The

Loyalists must realize they're outnumbered, because no one else argues.

"Dunmore has left Williamsburg men defenseless," Captain Brandon continues, "but my men have come to your aid. We are ready to stand tall for all Virginians!"

"Huzzah!" people shout.

Being in the middle of the action makes me feel like a true Patriot, proud to demand independence and angry at anyone who gets in the way. "Huzzah!" I yell. "Huzzah!" I wait for the soldiers to lead a charge into the Palace. I will join right in!

But surprisingly, the noise behind us gradually dies down. "Hush," a woman standing next to us says. "Peyton Randolph is here!"

I lean close to Felicity. "Who is Peyton Randolph?" I ask.

"Why, he's a Patriot leader," she says. "He represents Virginia at the Continental Congress. Everyone admires Mr. Randolph, and respects him too."

A tall man is making his way toward Captain Brandon. Mr. Randolph carries a walking stick and looks quite elegant. Sunlight glints off the buckles on his black shoes and the buttons on his long plum-colored coat. His

black hat is trimmed with gold too. He wears a poufy lace scarf around his neck and a wig made with dark curls shaped like sausages. I've seen interpreters wear wigs when my dad and I visit Colonial Williamsburg, and I always think they look kind of dumb. But somehow Mr. Randolph makes it look good.

"Captain Brandon," he begins loudly but calmly, like he has all the time in the world. "There is no reason for your men to be here. I have come with a petition to present to the royal governor, asking for the return of our gunpowder."

We're so close that I can see Captain Brandon clench his fists. "Sir!" he says hotly. "The time for petitions is past. My men and I will demand what is rightfully ours!"

"We both want the return of our gunpowder," Mr. Randolph assures Captain Brandon. "But our cause will not be served by violence! We must find a way to demonstrate why we believe Governor Dunmore's actions are unfair."

Captain Brandon is so riled up that he stalks back and forth. "Governor Dunmore will not respect mere words!"

"It is our moral duty to try, and try again, and try yet again if we must." Mr. Randolph's voice is even stronger now. "Anger and bloodshed have never solved a problem."

I know, of course, that the Patriots did fight a war to win independence. Every July 4th the whole country celebrates winning the Revolutionary War, because that's what created the United States of America. If the Patriots had kept trying to make the British king understand their views by having meetings with British officials and talking about their frustrations and problems, would they have succeeded in becoming independent? Probably not, but . . . we'll never know.

"Our cause will not be served by this show of force," Mr. Randolph insists. "We must act with honor! Remember, Lady Dunmore and her children are inside the Palace."

"The governor has a family?" I murmur to Felicity. She nods soberly. Suddenly I don't feel like storming into the Palace anymore.

"My honor led me here, sir!" Captain Brandon insists. "This is the moment my men have trained for."

"The time when your skills are needed has not yet come," Mr. Randolph says. "Captain Brandon, please dismiss your company."

Felicity grabs my hand and squeezes it hard. I hold my breath. Captain Brandon hesitates. Finally, he nods.

Mr. Randolph turns and walks calmly toward the Palace. We all follow right behind him. Just as we reach the edge of the green, a servant in fancy clothes walks through the Palace gate and announces that Governor Dunmore will meet Mr. Randolph. I figure the meeting will be private, but instead—

"Gracious!" Felicity gasps. "It's the governor himself!"

Felicity and I slip to the front of the crowd to watch. The governor strides toward us. He wears tall gleaming boots and a scarlet coat with lots of gold trim. The young black servant and an elderly white man who must be some kind of assistant are with him, but I can't take my eyes off the governor. He looks totally furious.

"Explain yourself and this rabble, Mr. Randolph!" he snaps. "What is this threat against my home?"

I glance up at the Palace and see a curtain move

in a third-floor window. A small face appears against the glass. I nudge Felicity. "Look! Who is that?"

Felicity follows my gaze, squinting against the sun. "I think 'tis little Susan, the governor's daughter," she whispers back.

I imagine Susan watching her father face down an angry mob. If it were me, I'd be scared.

Mr. Randolph bows politely. "I am here to present your lordship with a petition," he calls, loud enough for us to hear. "I humbly request that you return our gunpowder."

The crowd is quiet. Everyone is leaning forward, straining to hear.

"I removed the gunpowder to keep it safe," the governor barks, "after hearing rumors of a slave uprising."

An angry rumble ripples through the crowd. "If you fear a slave revolt," somebody shouts, "it makes no sense to hide what we need to defend ourselves!"

Mr. Randolph shakes his head sorrowfully. "Lord Dunmore, I pray you restore our confidence."

The governor is silent for a long moment, as if he wants to remind us who is in charge. Finally, he says

in a snooty voice, "I will pay for the powder taken."

People start whooping like crazy. "The governor has given in! Huzzah!"

The governor stands like a statue, looking down his nose at the crowd. Mr. Randolph waves for everyone to pipe down. Gradually people get quiet again.

Governor Dunmore raises his voice. "But heed me well. I swear by God that if one grain of gunpowder is used against me or my family, I will arm your slaves with guns and burn Williamsburg to the ground."

Turn to page 42.

I figure it might be smart to get away from the angry crowd. "If you truly don't mind, I'd like to go to your house." I have to shout because it's so noisy on the street.

Felicity looks with longing toward the Governor's Palace one more time. Then she turns and smiles at me. "Of course," she says. "'Tis but a short walk."

"I'll walk with you as far as the store," Ben adds.

The streets get a little quieter as we leave the Palace behind, and I get my first good look at Williamsburg, 1775. Some things are the same as in the modern-day Williamsburg. Many of the buildings are familiar, and some of the people we pass don't look any different than interpreters wearing their costumes.

But there are differences, too. Bricklayers and carpenters are actually constructing some of the buildings that are old in my time. Some of the people on the streets wear clothes that are totally filthy and ragged. A few people seem to be speaking in other languages, and I wonder whether they are newly arrived immigrants. Instead of seeing just a few carriages and horseback riders in the streets, as I've seen when I've

visited Colonial Williamsburg with my dad, now I can't even count all the horse-drawn coaches, wagons pulled by oxen, and riders clogging the streets.

It even smells different now. Smoke rises from every chimney, the coaches kick up clouds of dust, and all those horses leave a lot of poop in the streets. When a man wearing a stained shirt and breeches bumps into me, I wrinkle my nose—I'm pretty sure he hasn't had a bath for a while. But there are some good smells, too. I inhale lavender perfume as a lady in a pretty dress hurries by. And the floury, sugary scent coming from a bakery makes my mouth water.

Felicity and Ben stop in front of a building that looks like a house. It's built of red bricks and has a steep, pointed roof.

"Oh!" I say. "Is this your father's store?"

Felicity looks proud. "'Tis the finest store in all of Virginia, I do believe!"

"I had best get inside," Ben says. "There are crates of glassware in the storeroom waiting to be unpacked." He nods politely at me and says, "Good day, miss," before hurrying up the steps.

Felicity watches him go with a wistful look. "If

you're not too hungry, we could stop inside," she suggests. "Would you like to see the store, or proceed to my house?"

To visit Merriman's Store, turn to page 35.

To walk on to Felicity's home, turn to page 61.

"It would be exciting to see the militia arrive," I say. Watch the American colonists stand up to the royal governor? Very cool.

Ben nods. "Be sure to stay close," he warns Felicity and me. "'Twould be easy to get lost."

The long green lawn in front of the Governor's Palace is filling with people. I see women carrying market baskets and men carrying leather satchels, as if they'd been running errands. Other people carry bricks and knives.

"What's happening?" an old lady asks. "Why is everyone gathering?"

"We must storm the Palace and take back our gunpowder!" a red-haired man shouts.

I can't help wondering whether I made a big mistake when I suggested we stay and watch. I glance at Felicity and Ben. They both look more excited than nervous, so I don't say anything.

"I hope the militia stays away altogether," a woman in a fancy blue dress says. She's twisting a handkerchief in her hands as if she's worried. "Threatening Governor Dunmore will only bring trouble to us all."

"The British are trampling on our rights!" another

woman insists. "Our men must fight to protect our freedom."

Most of the people gathering on the green are white, although I notice that some black people have clustered beneath a tree, murmuring among themselves. Maybe they are free, or maybe they are slaves running errands who have stopped to watch the commotion. What do they think when they hear Patriots shouting about freedom? I imagine they dream of liberty too.

We reach a little cluster of people surrounding a deeply tanned man dressed in stained and worn work clothes and a droopy felt hat. "You work for the governor," a lady says to the man, which is surprising, because he doesn't look like some royal servant. "What do you know of his plans?"

The man takes off his felt hat, and I realize that he's an Indian. He's shaved most of his head, but the long black hair left in the back is pulled into a ponytail decorated with one big feather.

"I know nothing of his plans," the man says with a shrug. "I've been away from Williamsburg on the governor's business, and just now returned." He walks on toward the Palace.

"Who was that?" I ask Ben.

"Governor Dunmore's Cherokee interpreter," he tells me. "The governor needs help communicating with the different Indian tribes."

"Four Shawnee men live at the Palace too," Felicity adds. "They came to Williamsburg after the governor made a treaty with the Shawnee tribe."

I've never really thought about Indians getting mixed up in the American Revolution. I want to ask what the Cherokee and Shawnee people think about the Patriots' plans for independence. But before I can open my mouth, a man behind us starts to shout. "Make way! Make way for Captain Brandon's militia company!"

Turn to page 40.

"I would love to see your father's store," I tell Felicity. We're here, so why not?

When we step inside, I pause to take it all in. Merriman's Store is very tidy, but there are all kinds of things for sale. Coffee beans and dried peas fill big open barrels. Bulging sacks look like they might hold flour or rice. Shelves behind the counters hold bolts of cloth, jars of spices, and tin coffeepots. Baskets, skillets, hoes, and other tools hang from the ceiling. Through an open door, I can see Ben working in the storeroom.

Felicity gestures toward a man behind the counter. "That's my father."

Mr. Merriman has ginger-colored hair and wears a handsome, dark blue coat. He's talking with a lady who wants to purchase chocolate. "My family is drinking more hot chocolate now that we're not drinking tea," she says.

Felicity leans close to murmur in my ear. "My father stopped selling tea months ago. 'Tis a way to protest the king's high taxes, which have made tea very expensive. But my father's decision made the Loyalists in town very angry! They stopped shopping

here." She sighs. "These are difficult times."

"Indeed," I say. That's what Ben said earlier when he agreed with Felicity about something.

"Still, many people continue to shop here," Felicity says.

I can tell that Felicity isn't a whiner. I like that about her. "Where do you get all these things to sell?" I wonder. There's more variety than I would have expected for 1775.

"Many things came from Great Britain," she explains.

I imagine sailors loading barrels and crates on a ship. "It must take months for things to arrive!"

"And once my father receives a shipment," Felicity says, "something might sit on a shelf for more months before a customer buys it."

It sounds as if Mr. Merriman sometimes has to pay for goods long before he actually sells them and makes a profit. He must have to plan very carefully.

When the customer leaves, Mr. Merriman beckons us over. Felicity explains that I traveled to Williamsburg with my father but lost him in the crowd.

"How do you do, sir?" I say.

"Your father is a Patriot, come to town like so many others?" Mr. Merriman asks.

I picture my dad in the costume he wears at Colonial Williamsburg. "Yes, sir. He is a Patriot." And it's funny, but even though Dad is just playacting, suddenly I feel proud of him. I know enough about the American Revolution to know that the Patriots were very brave to stand up to the British king and his mighty army. Now my dad helps visitors learn about what happened.

"Well, there's much to occupy a man in town today," Mr. Merriman says. "I trust you'll be reunited once the speeches and musters are done."

"I'm sure we will," I say.

He looks at Felicity. "Lissie, I have an important delivery to make, and I'll need Ben's help. Will you mind the shop for a short while? We won't be gone long."

Felicity stands a little taller. "Of course, Father!"

Once we're alone, Felicity hurries behind the counter. "'Tis a rare treat to mind the store," she says happily. "Mother wants me to stay home and practice stitching and such. I'm learning how to be ladylike, but sometimes . . ." Her secret smile makes me feel as

if we've been friends forever. "Sometimes I'm ready to weep from boredom."

I laugh as I follow Felicity. Then my eye catches a china tea set displayed on the counter. It's white with blue flowers. I'm pretty sure my grandmother has a platter with that pattern in her antiques shop. Wouldn't she love to see this set!

"This china is beautiful," I say.

"It is," Felicity agrees. "It was displayed on a high shelf for months, but no one purchased it. Just yesterday I helped my father arrange it here in hopes it might catch a customer's fancy."

I step sideways so I won't accidentally knock one of the delicate cups or bowls to the floor. Then I smile, pretending I am the shopkeeper. All I've ever done in my grandma's shop is dust or run the vacuum cleaner. But now it's just me and Felicity, in charge of a Patriot's store. This will be fun, I think. Visiting 1775 makes everything I've studied in school so real!

But before we can help a single customer, a black-haired boy about Ben's age bursts into the shop. He looks around wildly. "Where is Mr. Merriman?"

Felicity looks perplexed. "Why—my father and

Ben are making a delivery," she says. "Gracious, Eli! Whatever is the matter?"

"I've come to warn you," Eli says. He struggles to catch his breath. "You've got trouble on the way!"

Turn to page 50.

Everyone shuffles backward to clear a space down the middle of the green. Somebody tromps on my foot, but I hardly notice. I'm on tiptoes trying to catch a glimpse of the soldiers.

"Oh, look!" Felicity claps her hands in excitement as a column of men comes into view, marching down the green toward us. There must be fifty or more. Most of them wear fringed leather buckskins like frontier explorers. Some don't look any older than Ben, and a few have white hair. Some march and some just trudge along. Honestly, they don't look like soldiers. But they all carry muskets and seem ready for a fight.

"I so envy those men," Ben murmurs.

Felicity looks troubled. "Don't forget you are an apprentice—" she begins.

"Ben!" someone calls, and I see a skinny young man sliding through the crowd nearby. He's moving fast, but he stops and claps Ben on the shoulder.

"Good day, Ezra." Ben introduces Felicity and me before waving an arm toward the militia, "'Tis an exciting day, aye?"

Ezra looks around, as if checking to see whether anyone is paying attention to him. He's tied a bright

blue cloth over his black curls instead of wearing a hat. When he turns, I notice the hatchet hanging from a cord tied around his waist.

"Listen close!" Ezra hisses. "The real excitement is elsewhere. Some say that the British marines sent by Governor Dunmore didn't steal all the gunpowder from the Magazine, but instead left several barrels behind. I'm gathering a few true Patriots to fetch out the remaining barrels before the governor sends more marines to steal them, too. Are you with us?"

"Indeed I am!" Ben exclaims eagerly. Then he seems to remember that he's not on his own. "What say you, Felicity?" he asks. "Will you come with us to the Magazine?"

Felicity hesitates. "Oh, Ben, I don't know." She turns to me and whispers, "Part of me wants to go, but it could be dangerous. What say you?"

❀ ***To stay at the Palace, turn to page 22.***

❀ ***To go seize the remaining gunpowder, turn to page 44.***

A shiver slides down my back like an ice cube. Even though I know Williamsburg doesn't get burned down, it's terrible to hear that threat.

Mr. Randolph acts as if he didn't even hear the warning. "Thank you, sir."

"We are done here," the governor snaps. He turns and stomps back through the gate. His assistant accepts Mr. Randolph's petition before following the governor into the Palace. The servant follows. His face is like a mask, showing no expression.

Somebody raises another cheer. "To the tavern!"

Several men charge off. Other people stand around, chattering about what just happened. Two women nearby talk in worried tones. "Arming the slaves would lead to an uprising!" one exclaims.

"Surely the governor only made that threat because he was frightened for his family's safety," the other says. The women walk away, and we can't hear any more.

My brain is spinning. I mean, at first I was ready to charge into the Palace! Now, though, I'm glad Mr. Randolph was able to calm down the angry soldiers and the citizens who were ready to throw bricks through windows and generally go nuts. What would

have happened to the little girl I saw in the window if the soldiers had broken into the Palace?

I'm ready to be out of the crowd. "Well," I say, "I guess that's it. Felicity, shall we go to your house?"

She shakes her head. "I'm too worried about my friend Elizabeth and her family. Let us go back to their home. Perhaps someone will come to the door this time."

I totally understand. If Amara and Lauren were here, and they were Loyalists, I'd want to make sure they were okay, too.

I keep thinking about the different ways that Captain Brandon and Mr. Randolph acted, and how things turned out. Part of me wants to hang around and find out what will happen next. Being here is better than a whole year of social studies! But part of me wants to go straight back to my own time, and talk to my dad.

To go home,
turn to page 55.

To stay in Williamsburg with Felicity,
turn to page 69.

Why stay here and watch when we can go to the Magazine and take action? Ben and Felicity are true Patriots, and in all this excitement, I've become a true Patriot, too. I feel it in my heart. It makes me proud. "Let's go to the Magazine!" I say.

Ben grins. "Good!" Ezra says. "Let's go."

We move away from the Palace like fish swimming upstream. What would Dad say if he could see me heading off to the Magazine? Actually, I know exactly what he'd say. He'd order me to get home right this minute!

But Dad isn't here. I am in charge, and I don't need his permission to join the raid on the weapons storehouse. My skin feels all prickly with excitement.

At the end of the long green lawn we turn left. Soon we reach the Magazine, which is a three-story brick tower with a tall brick wall around it. Six or seven young men are lingering at the edge of the big grassy lawn surrounding the Magazine. "Those are our boys," Ezra says.

"Have you a plan?" Felicity asks eagerly.

Before Ezra can answer, a brown-haired man stomps up and grabs his arm. He wears a stained canvas apron over his clothes, and a pencil stub

is tucked behind one ear. "What mischief are you about?" he demands angrily. "An apprentice like you can't leave the shop without my permission!"

Ezra jerks his arm free. "Master Griffith, surely you can see that learning to make a board lie flat is hardly of consequence with such important matters being decided in Williamsburg. Why, we may soon be at war!"

"What I see are work orders stacking up." Master Griffith rubs a hand over his face. "You promised me seven years of work in return for teaching you the joiner's trade. In just three weeks, you've sorely tested my patience!"

"Then you are well rid of me," Ezra replies.

"Ezra, lad, think sharp," Master Griffith tries. "I'm known by all as a fair master. I feed and clothe my apprentices and treat them as members of my own family. You may never find so sweet a situation again. Come with me now, or I will be forced to throw our agreement in the fire. You will be left without provision of any kind."

I can tell that Master Griffith means what he says—and I have to admit, it only seems fair, if Ezra breaks his promise.

But Ezra doesn't seem to care about his apprenticeship. "Burn the agreement," he says defiantly. "I have no wish to learn the joiner's trade anyway. 'Twas my father's plan. I will make my own decisions!"

Master Griffith scowls. "I am quit of you, then, and glad of it." Yet, as he turns to go, I hear him mutter to himself, "But in all this turmoil, where will I find another apprentice?"

"Was that wise, Ezra?" Felicity asks. She casts a worried glance at Ben, as though she's afraid Ezra might give him bad ideas. "What will you do?"

"I will become a soldier," Ezra says. "But first, I will retrieve the remaining barrels of gunpowder from the Magazine and give them to the Patriot leaders! Are you still with me?"

"We are indeed," Ben assures Ezra.

We join the waiting group of young men. Most look as if they work hard for a living, although a couple are dressed in fancy clothes.

"The plan is simple," Ezra tells us. "The guard told me not an hour ago that he is sympathetic to our cause. When we approach, he will pretend to be overwhelmed by our numbers and will let us pass."

Looking around, I see faces filled with fierce anger and determination. Some boys are quivering with excitement, like dogs straining to be let off the leash. Many carry hatchets or knives.

What have I gotten myself into?

"Look for the remaining barrels of gunpowder," Ezra continues. "There's transportation already waiting." He points toward a horse-drawn cart parked near the Magazine. The driver sits with elbows resting on knees, holding a mug, and looking for all the world like he's just taking a coffee break.

"What about the guns?" someone demands. "I've heard there are three thousand flintlock muskets inside!"

"Governor Dunmore stole only our gunpowder, so we by rights will take only what gunpowder remains," Ezra tells him sternly. "We will not become common thieves."

I like the way Ezra is thinking so far, but suddenly he turns to Felicity and me. "What we're about is no work for girls. You will stay outside."

"We can help!" Felicity protests.

"'Tis best that you do not," Ben murmurs. "I'd have

to answer to your father, Felicity, should you get hurt."

Felicity hesitates, but finally nods. "Very well. We'll wait here."

Ben and the other young men stalk across the lawn like a pack of wolves. "Why are so many weapons stored there, anyway?" I ask Felicity.

"Citizens must be able to protect themselves against danger of any kind," she explains. "Indian attacks, slave revolts—even pirate raids."

Pirates? But before I can ask about pirates, a girl steps in front of us. She's maybe a year or two older than me, but it looks as if life has been hard on her. Her white cap is dirty. She's tucked the hem of her skirt into her waistband, revealing a grimy petticoat. Her cracked shoes are tied closed with twine. Worst of all, there's a pinched, hungry look on her face.

Still, she greets us with a determined smile. "You two pretty misses need posies." She reaches inside the pouch she's made of her skirt and pulls out two limp bunches of pansies and violets tied with string. "Perfect for spring, and they cost only—"

"I'm truly sorry," Felicity interrupts, looking sympathetic, "but I don't have any money."

"Me either," I add. I wish I could help the girl, but I don't know how. She looks disappointed, and turns away.

I glance back toward the raiders. They've reached the gate in the wall.

"I can't see!" Felicity complains, rising on her tiptoes.

"Ben didn't say we had to stay way over here," I point out. "Let's go closer."

"Aye, let's," she agrees.

We reach the wall just as Ben and the others shove through the gate. "Now that they're inside the wall we still can't see," I mutter. "If only—"

A loud explosion shivers through the air. Then another.

My heart zooms into hyperdrive. Felicity grabs my hand, her eyes wide with alarm. "That was gunfire!"

Turn to page 58.

I don't like the sound of this. Maybe actually visiting 1775 is making things too real. Felicity and I share a worried glance.

"I've just come from my master's shop," Eli continues. "Some Committee of Safety men are visiting all the stores in Williamsburg. They're on their way here."

Committee of Safety? That doesn't sound too bad.

"Surely they won't bring trouble," Felicity protests. "My father agreed not to sell tea, and he has not."

"But with so many people angry at the British because the governor stole our gunpowder, the committee men are feeling bold," Eli says. "They're warning storekeepers against selling *anything* from Great Britain."

"Anything?" Felicity echoes.

Eli nods. "I must be on my way." He hurries out the door, and we see him race off.

Felicity and I are alone in the shop again, but pretending to be in charge isn't fun anymore. "Felicity, what is the Committee of Safety, anyway?"

She looks surprised. "I thought everyone knew! But I forget, news can be hard to come by outside of Williamsburg."

"Indeed," I say again. It's a handy word.

"The king requires storekeepers in the colonies to buy almost all of their wares from Great Britain," Felicity explains. "But some months ago, colonists who favor independence announced new rules."

"What kind of rules?" I ask.

"Storekeepers must find new sources of goods to sell. And my father is doing so. But . . ." Felicity makes a helpless gesture, taking in the many things on display. "He can't simply throw away everything he'd already purchased from Great Britain!"

That makes sense to me. Without selling what is already on his shelves, Mr. Merriman won't have any money to buy new goods made in the American colonies.

"Maybe we should close the shop and lock the doors until your father returns," I suggest.

Felicity sucks in her lower lip, thinking. Finally she shakes her head. "My father has no argument with the committee. If he hasn't returned by the time the men arrive, I shall hear them out and pass their message along."

I'm not sure I like that plan, but I'm in no position to

argue. "Maybe Eli was exaggerating," I say hopefully.

Then I hear feet clomping heavily on the front steps. A man strides in, followed by three—no, four—more. One is quite elderly, with long white hair. Two are barely in their twenties. Three wear fancy outfits, and the others look like farmers. The only thing these men have in common is a grim expression.

The first man steps to the door to the storeroom and looks back there. "No sign of Merriman," he mutters to his friends.

I'm too nervous to speak. But not Felicity! She lifts her chin. "Good day, gentlemen," she says. "How may I help you?"

"Where's Merriman?" the man demands. It takes all my courage not to step backward.

One of the other men elbows him. "Have a care, Jack," he scolds. "'Tis but a child you're speaking to."

Jack looks irritated, but he does try again. "Beg pardon, miss. Where is Mr. Merriman?"

"My father is making a delivery," Felicity says. "Is there some news you would like me to give him?"

"Since the royal governor stole our gunpowder," Jack says, "it is necessary for merchants to send a

strong message to the king. Your father must stop selling any goods made in Great Britain. Immediately."

"My father no longer sells tea," Felicity says, "and he is trying to—"

"Trying is not good enough!" Jack snaps. He looks around. "I see some British goods here."

One of the other men turns to a shelf piled high with neatly folded fabric. "I believe this cloth is British," he says. He pulls the fabric from the shelf and lets it fall to the floor.

Felicity's eyes go wide. "What are you *doing?*"

The man dances a little jig right on the cloth. His shoes are rough and dirty. Jack laughs. One of the young men claps his hands.

I open my mouth, but no sound comes out.

Another man uses one arm to swipe the pretty china I'd been admiring from the counter. Every single piece! They fall to the floor with a terrible crash. Bits of broken plates and cups scatter.

"Stop it!" Felicity cries.

I watch in horror, thinking of Mr. Merriman, who will never be able to sell that lovely china set now. I also think about how much my grandmother would

treasure even a single teacup from 1775.

The elderly man says quietly, "That's enough, now."

But Jack isn't ready to quit. He grabs a book and begins tearing out pages. "We've got enough to start a bonfire," he says. "What think you, friends?"

"*Stop!*" Felicity shrieks. Her eyes look glassy. I can tell she's trying not to cry.

And suddenly, I've just had it with these bullies. I storm around the counter. "Shame on you!"

Jack laughs. "We're doing Merriman a favor. No Patriot will shop at a store that sells British goods."

Felicity said earlier that Loyalists have already stopped shopping at Merriman's store. If the Patriots stop coming here too, the store will go out of business! And if Felicity or I can't figure out how to stop these men from destroying things, Mr. Merriman won't have anything to sell to anyone.

Then I remember something else Felicity said.

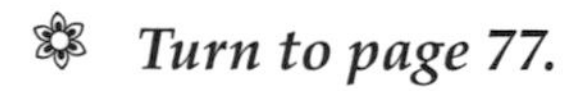
Turn to page 77.

elicity," I say, "I need to go. I—I think I saw my father across the green."

"I'll come with you!" she offers.

I shake my head. "No, thank you. I'll be fine." I start to walk away. Then I turn back and hug Felicity. "You've been really nice," I tell her. "I'll always remember you."

"Good luck," she says. "I hope you find your father."

I do too, I think, as I begin squeezing through the crush of people. I hope I can find the *old* dad. The dad I had before Mom got so sick and died.

Once I'm away from the crowd, I scoot behind a tall fence and pull the miniature painting from beneath the kerchief. I take a deep breath, look into the lady's eyes . . . and before I know it, I'm back in my grandma's antiques shop.

I help Grandma make dinner, and I think about what happened in front of the Palace. I keep hearing Mr. Randolph's voice in my head: Instead of fighting, we must find a way to demonstrate why we believe Governor Dunmore's actions are unfair.

I've been more and more frustrated with my dad's rules lately. When he treats me like a baby, I get mad at

him. I've complained about it, and tried to get him to change his mind. But maybe I haven't done the best job of explaining how the rules make me feel.

When Dad gets home, the first thing he says is, "What a day." He sounds tired. He looks tired, too. Although I've been practicing what I want to say in my head, I almost chicken out. Maybe I should put it off until a better time.

But I've already waited too long to tell him about things. "Dad," I begin, as Grandma sets his dinner in front of him. "Can I talk to you?"

Dad sighs. "Can it wait? I'm beat."

"It's really important," I tell him.

"Why don't I leave you two alone," Grandma murmurs, and slips from the room.

Dad sprinkles Parmesan cheese over his spaghetti. "What's on your mind?"

I take a deep breath. "I am very frustrated by some of the rules around here. I really, really wanted to go to the animal shelter with Lauren and Amara."

"I can't let you go places with people I don't know," Dad says flatly.

There's nothing dangerous about going to an animal

shelter! I want to shout—but I don't. Instead I tell him, "Well, I have some ideas about that. First, since Lauren and Amara are my best friends, can we set up a pizza party or something? So all the parents can meet?"

"That," Dad says, "is an excellent idea."

"Great," I say. "But Dad?" I take a deep breath. "I also need to tell you that sometimes you make me feel like you don't trust me to make good choices."

Dad puts his fork down, but he doesn't say anything. My heart is pounding. Is he mad?

✿ ***Turn to page 65.***

The gunshots are still echoing in my ears as one of the raiders staggers through the gate. Blood trickles down his face. His linen shirt is splotched with blood. Another boy appears behind him, one hand clamped over the opposite shoulder. I can see a blood-stain growing beneath his fingers.

I taste something sour. This isn't even a little bit fun anymore. "What happened?" I cry.

"Someone set a booby trap!" the boy says. He sounds dazed. His knees buckle, and he sits down hard on the ground.

"Where is Ben?" Felicity cries. The boy doesn't answer.

More boys stumble through the gate, but there's no sign of Ben. A new crowd is forming as people who heard the gunfire run to see what happened.

"Ben?" I call, looking wildly about. "Ben, where are you?" A hand seems to be squeezing my heart. Is Ben badly hurt? Is he . . . is he dead?

Felicity looks frantic. "I don't see him anywhere!"

I cast one last look around, desperately wanting to see Ben. Maybe even wishing I could spot my dad in the crowd. He'd know what to do.

"Ben must still be inside," Felicity says. She plunges through the gate. I'm right behind her.

A narrow yard circles the Magazine. And—there's Ben, on his knees beside Ezra, who is collapsed on the ground. The figures blur as tears of relief fill my eyes, and I blink hard. I don't see any blood on Ben's clothes, but Ezra looks badly hurt.

Felicity and I dart over. "How can we help?" Felicity asks at once. I'm not thinking clearly, so I'm glad she is.

"Bandages," Ben orders. "Quickly!"

"Step out of your petticoat," Felicity tells me. She reaches under her skirt and drops hers easily, then helps me when my hands fumble with the button. Ben folds one petticoat against the bloody spot in Ezra's side. Then he tears strips from the other petticoat to tie the bandage in place. "You'll be all right," he tells his friend.

"What happened?" I ask.

"Someone rigged two trap guns to fire as soon as anyone stepped inside the Magazine," Ben says grimly. "Those at the front were met with a shower of lead. 'Twas the governor's work, no doubt!"

I can hear a growing clamor of angry voices beyond

the wall. Ben tips his head, and I can tell he's listening too. "Ezra, let's get you outside," he says. "Lean on me."

Together we get Ezra to his feet and help him stagger through the gate. And just in time, too. More men are running across the lawn. The crowd is growing, and the mood is ugly.

"By God, this is beyond tolerance!" one man shouts.

"Blood has been spilled in Williamsburg!" bellows another.

A short man climbs up on a crate, waving his arms. "There are hundreds of muskets inside that Magazine. Pistols and swords and pikes, too. They were purchased with public funds and do not belong to Dunmore! Who will follow me into the Magazine to take what is rightfully ours?"

Turn to page 67.

I would like to see your home," I tell Felicity. What an amazing opportunity—especially since I'm going to be a junior interpreter this summer, helping Colonial Williamsburg's visitors learn about kids' lives.

The Merrimans' house is white clapboard with cheery yellow trim. Like most of the buildings in Williamsburg, it looks orderly and balanced, with the same number of windows on each side of the door and the same size flower gardens on each side of the walk, surrounded by a white picket fence. Inside, the house is quiet, and a pretty little girl is sitting in the parlor sewing.

"This is my sister Nan," Felicity says, and introduces me.

"I am pleased to meet you," Nan says. She has a shy, sweet smile.

"Where is everyone else?" Felicity asks her. "And why are you huddled inside?"

"I must stay where I can hear William when he wakes." Nan looks at me.

Felicity leans close and tells me, "William's only three. He still takes naps."

"Mother is out back, talking to Marcus," Nan continues. "She wants him to dig a new garden."

"Come along," Felicity tells me. "My mother will want to meet you." As we go back outside, she whispers, "I don't know how Nan can bear being so quiet and patient all the time."

I can't help laughing. Then I remember I'm about to meet Mrs. Merriman, so I get serious. I smooth my smudged skirt, hoping I don't make too bad an impression.

"Is Marcus another brother?" I ask as we round a corner of the house.

"Oh, no," Felicity says. "Marcus helps my father with heavy work, sometimes here and sometimes at the store."

Looking ahead, I realize my mistake. A lovely woman who must be Felicity's mother is talking to a handsome black man with close-cropped hair. He's holding a shovel. "Yes, mistress," I hear him say.

My feet stop moving. A thought shoots through me like lightning. "Felicity," I whisper. "Is Marcus a slave?"

"Why, yes." Felicity's forehead wrinkles. I can tell she doesn't understand why I stopped walking. "He's

been with my family for as long as I can remember."

We've studied slavery in school, so I know that in 1775, many white people owned black people. I know that tobacco was the most important crop in colonial Virginia, and that black slaves did most of the hard work in the fields. And we learned a little bit about how horrible slavery was.

My mouth feels dry, and I swallow hard as I glance back at Marcus. He wears nice clothes and looks as if he has plenty to eat. Mrs. Merriman is speaking quietly to him, not screaming. But nothing can change the fact that Marcus is not free.

"Are you well?" Felicity asks with a look of concern. "'Tis a warm day. Shall I fetch you a drink of water?"

"Yes, please," I say. When Felicity hurries away, I step back around the corner, out of sight from the garden. I need to think really hard about being here, because suddenly it's making me very uncomfortable. All I wanted to do was have an adventure! I wanted to spend time with Felicity and learn about life in colonial Virginia. It had never occurred to me that I'd meet an enslaved man at the Merrimans' house.

I don't know what to do. Part of me thinks I should

stay, even though it's upsetting. I'll do a better job as a junior interpreter if I learn about everything I can—even terrible things. But another part isn't sure I can bear it.

You better make a decision quick, I tell myself, because Felicity will be back any minute.

To return to modern times, turn to page 87.

To stay in 1775, turn to page 74.

65

Dad," I continue hesitantly, "I've been wondering if I could do something to prove that I'm not a little kid anymore. Maybe I could volunteer to walk dogs or clean cages at the animal shelter. If I can do that, and still get my homework done, and chores . . ." I seem to run out of words. I hope Dad understands what I'm trying to say.

For a long time, he doesn't speak. *He just doesn't get it,* I think.

But then he blows out a long sigh. "You're right, Pumpkin. Maybe I have been too strict with you."

I can hardly believe my ears.

"If I have," Dad continues slowly, "it's because I love you and want to keep you safe. Ever since your mom died . . ."

"I know," I say. Suddenly I have a salty lump in my throat.

Dad coughs as if he has a lump in his throat, too. "I like your idea, though. Let's stop by the animal shelter together and get you set up for volunteer training. If you are responsible enough to manage volunteer work and homework for a month, we can adjust some of the rules. Does that sound fair?"

"Yes," I tell him. "That sounds fair."

I can hardly believe it. I didn't think there was anything I could do to get Dad to change some of his rules. But Mr. Randolph was right. Sometimes a conversation can do more good than all kind of complaints and arguments.

Dad glances at the wall clock. "We might have time to go to the shelter yet tonight if you want to ask about volunteer work. I know this is important. Maybe you can see the puppy Lauren picked out, too."

I consider, then shake my head. "Tomorrow will be good," I tell him. "I want to work on my persuasive essay about citizenship tonight." I haven't known what to write about, but all of a sudden, I have some ideas.

"Choosing to work on homework instead of going to the animal shelter?" Dad's eyebrows rise. "You are officially no longer a little kid."

He grins, and I grin. Then I clear our plates, open my books, and start on my essay.

The End

To read this story another way and see how different choices lead to a different ending, go back to page 43.

67

The crowd answers with an approving roar. A new tide of men surges toward the Magazine.

"Let's get away from here," Ben mutters. "Ezra's wounds need tending."

It isn't easy to back away. We're in the middle of a sea of furious shouts and shoving hands and scowling faces. Ezra groans a few times as he's jostled.

When we reach the street, I glance over my shoulder. Men are coming out of the Magazine waving guns and swords and the long spiky weapons I think are called pikes. One man hurls a drum on the ground and stomps on it. Several dance around as they rip a British flag to shreds. Stones fly through the air.

Crack! Crack-crack! More gunshots sound. I don't see any British soldiers coming to put a stop to this—at least not yet—so I can only imagine that the guns are being fired just to rile the crowd.

A woman screams. Feet pound as more people run back and forth—some trying to get closer, some trying to get away. A girl scurries by with her arms held over her head. An old man stands with a bloodstained handkerchief pressed to one cheek, looking confused. A burly man in a leather shirt knocks down the girl

who'd been selling flowers. He doesn't even look back.

"I have to take care of Ezra," Ben says urgently.

"We'll help you," Felicity says.

"But 'tis not safe for you girls to be out and about," Ben argues. "Please, Felicity, get clear of this mob. You and your friend should go home."

Felicity gets a stubborn look in her eye. I can tell that she isn't ready to go home. But while I admire her bravery, I'm not sure I feel the same way.

- ***To stay in 1775, turn to page 86.***

- ***To return to modern times, turn to page 119.***

ay I accompany you to your friend's house?" I ask Felicity.

"Of course!" Felicity assures me. "You will like Elizabeth. The Coles are Loyalists, but that doesn't mean they aren't nice people."

Felicity leads me to the Coles' house, which is a few blocks away. She knocks firmly, and a servant comes to the door.

"Please tell Miss Elizabeth and her mother that I've come to call," Felicity says. "I wish to make sure they are well."

The servant lets us inside, and we only wait a few moments before she leads us into a parlor. A woman and a pretty girl are sitting together. The girl jumps up when we walk in. "Oh, Felicity!" she cries. "'Tis good to see you."

Felicity introduces me to Elizabeth and her mother, and I bend my knees in a curtsy. "I am pleased to meet you."

"You girls are welcome here," Elizabeth's mother says kindly, "but I fear you should be safely home."

"We've haven't dared leave the house," Elizabeth adds. She looks really stressed. "Not with so many

people threatening all Loyalists with harm! Did the militia break into the Palace?"

"No," Felicity tells her. "Mr. Randolph managed to calm everyone down. He told the militia to disband."

Mrs. Cole closes her eyes for a few seconds. "Thank goodness," she says. "I feared—"

Before she can finish, the servant returns. "Excuse me, ma'am. Mrs. Hutchinson and Mrs. Kipling have come."

"Gracious," Mrs. Cole murmurs. "'Tis hardly a day for guests." But after smoothing her skirt, she speaks so calmly you'd never guess she feels frazzled. "Please show them in."

The servant ushers two elegant ladies into the parlor. They both wear fancy skirts that are pushed way out on the sides but flat in front. They also wear big wigs. I'm pretty sure the idea is that the richer you are, the bigger the wig. One lady's wig is brown, and the other lady's wig is powdered a pale pink. A fine dust of pink powder has landed on her shoulders, too, but we all pretend not to notice.

Elizabeth, Felicity, and I bob little curtsies. "Good day, friends," Mrs. Cole says.

“I’m afraid we’re not here for a social call,” the brown-wigged lady says. “You are surely aware that a mob threatened the Palace today?”

Elizabeth’s mother nods. “’Tis a sad day, Mrs. Hutchinson. These young ladies were just telling us what happened.”

“We can all imagine how terrified Lady Dunmore and her children must be,” the pink-wigged woman adds. “So Mrs. Hutchinson and I have decided to pay her a call. We must prove that not everyone in Williamsburg means them harm. Will you join us?”

Mrs. Cole looks shocked. “Approach the Palace without an invitation?”

“The nature of our call is more important than anything else.” Mrs. Kipling raises her chin. I can tell she’s not used to people questioning her judgment.

“Lady Dunmore likely will not be available to greet us,” Mrs. Hutchinson adds. “I expect we’ll give our names to the footman and that will be that. But by making the attempt to visit the governor’s wife, we will demonstrate that she has not lost our affection.”

Mrs. Kipling nods. “And you must bring your daughter.” She looks at Elizabeth. “What say you, child?”

Elizabeth takes a step sideways so her shoulder touches Felicity's. "Me?"

"'Tis not a formal occasion," Mrs. Hutchinson assures her. "It's unlikely you'll so much as glimpse Lady Dunmore."

Elizabeth licks her lips. "Might Felicity come? And her new friend?"

Mrs. Kipling looks at me. I feel my eyes go wide. Visit the Palace? Me?

"My eldest daughter is away," Mrs. Cole says. "And I'm sure 'twould help put the governors' children at ease if several young people are in attendance."

I'm pretty sure Mrs. Kipling would rather I didn't come. She's probably not thrilled about Felicity going either. But she gives in. "Oh, very well. We shall call for you in two hours."

After Mrs. Kipling and Mrs. Hutchinson leave, the parlor gets real quiet. Mrs. Cole looks stunned. Elizabeth looks overwhelmed.

Felicity looks like she doesn't know what to do. Still, she remembers that I must be more freaked out than anybody. "You needn't go if you don't wish to," she murmurs.

Fifteen minutes ago I was ready to charge through the Palace gate with a group of soldiers. Now it seems that if I want to, I can walk through that same gate as a guest!

Mrs. Cole takes a deep breath and smiles at me. "What would you like to do?"

To visit the Palace, turn to page 81.

To decline the invitation, turn to page 101.

I'm *staying*, I decide. I want to learn as much as I can about colonial days—good and bad and everything in between.

I hear Felicity's footsteps, so I walk back around the corner. She brings a tin cup filled with cool water and watches with concern as I sip. "Does that help?"

"Yes, thank you," I say. "I'm better now."

Mrs. Merriman leaves Marcus and joins us. Felicity explains that I lost my father in the crowd.

"Dear me," Mrs. Merriman says. "He must be worried."

"Oh, probably not," I say quickly, because I don't want her to freak out. "He's a Patriot, ma'am. He might even march off with the militia."

"And what of your mother, child?" Mrs. Merriman asks. She looks tired and worried, but her eyes are filled with kindness.

"My mother died last year," I tell her.

"I'm very sorry." She gently strokes a strand of hair away from my face. "And I greatly fear these troubles brewing between the colonies and King George will bring more hardship upon too many girls like yourself."

It's true, I think sadly. The Revolutionary War lasted a long time, and many soldiers were killed. Lots of women and children had to make do on their own.

"I knew I should bring her home, Mother," Felicity says. "She's in need of refreshment. And her dress . . ."

"Of course." Mrs. Merriman smiles at me. "You and Felicity look to be about the same size. You can wear her spare dress while we tidy your own."

Before we can go inside, however, we see that Marcus has come to stand a short distance away. "Pardon, mistress," he says to Mrs. Merriman. "Have you decided whether you want me to bring out the carriage?"

"The carriage?" Felicity's eyebrows shoot high with surprise. "Mother, are you traveling?"

"I am considering it," she admits. "It might be best if I take all of you children to King's Creek."

"King's Creek is my grandfather's plantation," Felicity tells me. "We always spend the summer there. Father visits when he can leave the store, and I do love being in the country!" She looks back at her mother. "But we've never left this early before."

"We've never had such unrest in Williamsburg

before, Lissie," her mother says. "Patriot militias are coming into the city, and I've heard rumors of British troops marching from the coast. I am anxious."
Mrs. Merriman turns to me. "If we go to King's Creek, you are most welcome to travel with us," she says.

- *To stay in Williamsburg, turn to page 131.*

- *To travel to King's Creek Plantation, go online to* **beforever.com/endings**

clench my fists and yell, "Stop this right now!" in my loudest soccer field voice.

The men are so surprised that they actually freeze. I guess they've never heard a colonial girl holler like that. The shop gets quiet.

I know I have to talk fast. "You're not being fair. You're not respecting your own rules!"

Some of the men look confused. "You're speaking nonsense," Jack growls.

"No, I'm not," I insist. "Patriots decided that merchants can no longer buy goods from the British, right? And named a date when that change would take place?"

One of the men shifts his weight from one foot to the other. "Aye, we did," he admits. "The new rule began this January past."

"Well, Mr. Merriman's goods don't always sell quickly," I inform him. "Some of these things have been on display for months. It's not fair to punish Mr. Merriman for trying to sell things he purchased from the British before January."

The men look at one another. "The lass makes a fair point," one of them admits.

I glance over my shoulder and see Felicity blinking

her tears away. She gives me a tiny nod: *Keep going!*

I look back at the men. "Mr. Merriman moved that china set from a high shelf to the counter because he's had it for a long time. He was trying to attract a buyer. If someone had purchased the china, he would have had money to buy new goods from someone in Virginia. But now every piece is broken. Which one of you is going to pay for it?" I glare at the ringleader. "Mr. Jack?"

"Well, I—I didn't . . ." He coughs. "That is, I thought . . ."

Felicity crouches, grasps a big ledger, and thumps it onto the counter. "This is our account book," she says briskly. "I shall make note of the destroyed merchandise, and mark it to the Committee of Safety."

One of the well-dressed men looks down his nose at her. "There may have been a brief misunderstanding, but that doesn't change the facts," he says in a snooty tone. "We have the right to seize British goods. Can you prove which items were purchased before the new rule was put into place?"

"My father keeps excellent records," Felicity assures him. "We can go through the accounts item by item."

"Of course, that will take a long time . . ." I let my voice trail away. I hope that if Felicity and I can stall these men long enough, Mr. Merriman will return before they cause any more trouble.

"Enough is enough, lads," says the elderly man. His voice is louder this time, and more firm. "We don't have time to study months of accounts. Let's be gone."

Jack points a finger at Felicity. "Tell your father that we'll be watching," he says. But it sounds more like bluster than a threat now. He turns around and stomps out of the store.

The white-haired man is last to leave. "Well done," he tells us softly. "I hope you lasses are both true Patriots. We need the likes of you." Then he follows the others.

Felicity rushes around the counter and hugs me. "Oh, thank you! Those louts had me so addled I could scarcely think straight."

"Well, you spoke up first," I remind her. "For a while I was too scared to say a word."

"We did well together," Felicity declares.

"But . . . look at the mess." I stare with dismay at the dirty cloth, ruined book, and broken china on the floor.

"I am sorely tempted to leave this for my father to see," Felicity says. "But—'tis best we clean up. We might yet get more customers today, and we must greet them properly."

I crouch and carefully begin picking up shards of china. "You're right."

"I can't guess what further mischief those men might have made without your quick thinking." Felicity gathers up the dirty cloth in her arms, but she grins at me. "I can hardly wait to tell my father and Ben how you saved the day!"

I hesitate, keeping my gaze on the china. Part of me wants to stay in 1775 and discover what will happen next. But—now that the excitement is over—part of me also feels as if this would be a good time to slip away, return to my own time, and think about everything that happened this afternoon.

To stay at the store, turn to page 96.

To return home, turn to page 107.

I'm here to see as much as I can, right? I say, "Well, I guess I'd like to visit the Palace. That is . . . if you're really sure it's all right."

"I am sure," Mrs. Cole says, "but we must make haste!" She tips her head, looking at me thoughtfully. "I've been saving a lovely gown that my older daughter has outgrown. It's too large for Elizabeth, but I do believe it might fit you well."

"I shall need to change into the gown I wore to my dancing lesson," Felicity says.

"Yes, dear, run on home and explain everything to your mother," Mrs. Cole tells her. "If she gives you permission to accompany us, meet us back here."

I follow Felicity to the door. "Are you sure you want to visit the Palace?" I ask. "Maybe it's not such a good idea. Especially since—" I lean close and whisper, "you know. You're a Patriot."

"I am," Felicity agrees. "But I do want to show that although Patriots are angry about the stolen gunpowder, we mean no harm to the governor's family."

That makes sense to me, so I nod and wave her off.

Mrs. Cole leads us upstairs. After helping Elizabeth change into her best yellow dress, she turns to me. The

first thing she gives me is a skirt covered with embroidered flowers and vines. I step into it and immediately feel like a fine lady. "It's beautiful!"

"Indeed." Mrs. Cole smiles and reaches for another skirt. This one is white with little pink and green flowers printed on it, and has a top to match.

"Pardon, ma'am, but . . . do I need both skirts?" I ask.

Elizabeth giggles, then quickly presses a hand over her mouth and tries to pretend that she didn't. But I can tell she's not really making fun of me. "The first is a petticoat!" she explains.

I can hardly believe that somebody decorated a petticoat with so much embroidery. None of it will show! Honestly, it's prettier than the real skirt. But at least I get it now. I look from the petticoat to Elizabeth, and we both burst out laughing. I completely understand why she's Felicity's best friend. She's sweet and lots of fun.

"That's enough merriment, girls." Mrs. Cole slides the real skirt into place and laces me into the bodice. She also finds me a kerchief to match, and a white cap with lace and a pink bow.

"You look beautiful," Elizabeth tells me.

"Thank you," I say. The dress I'm wearing is not as fancy as Elizabeth's or the swishy blue dress Felicity shows up wearing, but that's okay. I love the way I look!

Mrs. Kipling and Mrs. Hutchinson return, and they lead the way to the Palace. It's a breezy day, and I keep smoothing my skirt, trying to look like a proper young lady. "Is there anything I need to know about visiting the Palace?" I ask Felicity in a low voice. I don't want to embarrass myself or my new friends.

"I've been learning about manners from Miss Manderly, my teacher," Felicity murmurs. "And I even once visited the Palace. But there are many, many rules about how proper young ladies must act." She looks half worried and half determined. "I don't know them all myself, so we must simply do the best we can."

The Palace green is mostly empty now, and no one looks twice as we approach the gate. I can't help feeling a bit trembly, and when I glance at Elizabeth and Felicity, I'm pretty sure they're feeling trembly too. I'm a Patriot at heart, but still—I've never been inside a Palace before. It's kind of overwhelming.

One servant greets us at the gate and escorts us to the door. Then another servant waves us into the

front hall. My jaw drops. The walls are covered with weapons. Muskets are mounted above the fireplace. Crossed swords hang from floor to ceiling. Handguns with long barrels are arranged in fans above the doors to other rooms.

The servant asks us to wait while she takes word of our arrival to Lady Dunmore. When we're alone, I whisper to Felicity, "What's with all the guns?"

Mrs. Kipling overhears. "The guns and swords are symbols of the governor's power and his responsibility to protect British subjects," she murmurs. "They are displayed as decoration, but in an emergency, they are instantly available."

"Can you imagine what would have happened if the militia, and the mob on the green earlier, had charged the Palace?" Mrs. Hutchinson asks. "The governor's men would surely have taken up weapons and fired."

Mrs. Kipling shudders. "Or—imagine if all these weapons had ended up in the hands of those troublemakers!"

Even though I am on the side of those trouble-makers, I have to admit, it's scary to imagine what

could have happened if angry men on either side had grabbed these weapons.

The servant returns. "Lady Dunmore will be honored to receive you in her sitting room." She turns around to lead the way.

For a moment, no one else moves. Elizabeth's eyes go round as saucers. Felicity sucks in her breath. Even the grown-ups look startled. I don't think anyone thought that the governor's wife would actually invite us into a private room!

Turn to page 115.

I want to get out of here—but since I was the one who suggested coming here in the first place, it doesn't seem right to run away now.

I glance away so I can think. Suddenly I notice the flower seller. She's crawled to the side of a building so she won't get trampled, and she's huddled there with her hands over her face. Her shoulders shake as if she's crying. Her pansies and violets got spilled and are crushed on the ground. I want to go see if she's okay. But Ezra is bleeding badly and needs care—fast.

A teenage boy runs past us, then stops. He was pounding toward the mob that's still ransacking the Magazine, but his sharp blue eyes move quickly from Ezra to Ben, taking in the situation in a flash. "Do you need aid?" he asks Ben.

If this guy helps, Ben won't need me and Felicity. Ben glances from her to me, a question in his eyes.

To help Ezra,
turn to page 104.

To help the girl who was knocked down,
turn to page 91.

My feet start moving again. This time I'm running—away from the garden and back to the street. I quickly get lost in the crowd. I hurry along until I find a quiet spot behind a big tree. I pull out the miniature and stare at the painted lady. Did you own other people? I ask her silently.

Then I have to close my eyes because the world is spinning, spinning, spinning me back to my own time. As soon as I find myself back in my grandmother's shop, I return the miniature painting to its case and hurry up the stairs.

"Is everything all right?" Grandma asks, as she ties on her apron.

"Yes," I say, even though it isn't. She gives me one of those *I don't believe you, but I'll let it go* looks. I feel better just being with her in this familiar kitchen.

Then I start thinking about Felicity, and how nice she was to me, and how rude it was to leave without even saying good-bye. My feelings are all tangled up.

I help Grandma make dinner. When it's ready, we eat spaghetti and salad without saying much. By the time my dad comes home, I'm pretending to do homework. Muffy, my mustard-colored cat, is curled up in my lap.

"I left your plate in the microwave, and there's salad in the fridge," Grandma tells him. "I'm going down to the shop for a while."

Dad zaps his plate of spaghetti and sits down across from me. "How's the homework coming, Pumpkin?"

I close my math book. "Can I talk to you about something?"

"Sure." He digs into his spaghetti.

Since I'm about to fib a little, I keep my gaze on Muffy. "I started writing a story about a colonial girl who lives in Williamsburg. I really like her! The character, I mean. The family isn't super rich, but they have nice things. To be true to history, would her parents have to own slaves? And if they did, wouldn't that mean they were . . ." It's hard to even say it. "Really bad people?"

"There's no excuse for slavery." Dad leans back in his chair. "But that doesn't mean the girl you've imagined can't be a nice person."

"Trying to understand people who owned slaves is really confusing," I confess.

"It can be," Dad agrees. "But as historians, our job is to discover what happened long ago."

Dad's never called me a historian before. I kind of like that.

"You have to think about your character in terms of the time and place where she grew up," Dad continues. "Life was very different in colonial days. Many white parents taught their children that it was all right to own enslaved workers. You can't think of your character, or judge her, as if she was raised in modern times. She can still help people and do good things."

That makes sense. I know Felicity has a good heart.

"I'm proud of you, Pumpkin," Dad says. "Slavery is a difficult thing to think about. But we must think about it, and help other people learn what happened. Having conversations like this is one of the reasons I like volunteering at Colonial Williamsburg."

"When I'm a junior interpreter, I'll try to help kids think about it, too," I promise.

"I bet you'll write a wonderful story, about a wonderful character who's just right for her time." He smiles. "And you're going to be a great junior interpreter."

Talking with my dad has made me feel better about some things. But I don't feel better about leaving 1775

without saying good-bye to Felicity.

Well, I think, that miniature painting is still down in the shop. If I tell Grandma I really, really love it, I'm pretty sure she'll let me keep it.

That settles it. Tonight, I'm going to do homework—that persuasive essay about citizenship I have to turn in on Monday. After visiting 1775 and talking with Dad, I have some new ideas.

But tomorrow, I'm going back in time. I can't free Marcus, but I can apologize to Felicity for disappearing the way I did.

I'm pretty sure she'll forgive me, and we'll be off on a new adventure.

The End

To read this story another way and see how different choices lead to a different ending, go back to page 31.

es, please," I quickly tell the guy who offered to help. I figure Ben can get Ezra to a doctor more quickly if he's got another strong boy to assist.

Felicity and I watch the three of them go on their way. Then I tip my head toward the flower seller. "Felicity, I'd like to see if there's anything we can do to help that girl."

"Aye, let's," Felicity says at once.

The girl has drawn up her knees and buried her face on her arms, so she doesn't notice when we approach. I touch her shoulder. "Pardon me."

Her head jerks up. "Oh!" she gasps, and swipes at her tear-stained cheeks. "I'll be on my way." She scrambles to her feet.

"We're not here to make you leave!" I exclaim.

"'Tis clear you've had a hard time today," Felicity adds. "We saw you get knocked down. May we walk you home?"

The girl just shakes her head.

"What's your name?" I ask.

"Sibyl," she says hesitantly. "Just Sibyl."

I'm not sure why she makes a point of saying "Just Sibyl," but Felicity guesses.

"Are you an indentured servant?" Felicity asks her.

Sibyl shrugs. "Maybe I once was."

"Did you run away?" Felicity asks softly.

"I'll not stay in any household where I'm beaten just for waking up in the morning." Sibyl looks defiantly from Felicity to me, as if daring us to argue.

I don't want to argue—I want to cry. When we learned about indentured servants in school, my teacher said that some had an okay time, but for many it was almost like slavery. "Can you go back to your parents, Sibyl?" I ask. "Surely they'd understand."

"I'm an orphan, you see. My father is dead." Sibyl shrugs as though it doesn't matter. But I can tell from the look in her eyes that it does.

My heart pinches tight, the way it always does when I think about my mom dying of cancer. "What about your mother?" I ask quietly.

"We'd really like to know," Felicity adds.

I can hear men still bellowing at the Magazine, and a dog barking, and somebody playing a fife. Sibyl hesitates again, and looks away as if she doesn't want to meet our eyes. Then she slides her right hand into a pocket that hangs around her waist. What has she got

hidden in there? "We just want to help," I tell her, trying to be encouraging.

Finally Sibyl pulls her hand from her pocket and displays a grubby scrap of cloth. It's tan with little blue flowers, and the edges are fraying.

Felicity and I look sideways at each other with the same silent message: *Do you understand? I don't.*

"This came from my mother," Sibyl explains. "She left me at the foundling home in London when I was a baby."

I'm not exactly sure what "foundling" means, but I'm pretty sure that a foundling home is some kind of orphanage.

"She told the people in charge that my father was dead, and she had no way to care for me." Sibyl stares off into the distance. "She also promised to come back for me. She tore this bit of cloth from her dress and left it as a token for the day she returned to claim me."

"But . . ." I can hardly form the words.

"My mother never came back," Sibyl says flatly. "I was trained to be a servant. And when I was seven, I was bound out to serve a family named Clarke. The Clarkes decided to come to the colonies, and they

brought me with them. But two years ago I grew tired of the beatings, and I ran away."

"I'm so sorry!" I put a hand on her arm. It just seems wrong that children like Sibyl basically get sold as servants.

"Nobody can make me go back to the Clarkes," Sibyl adds. "You'd never find them, anyway. They don't even live in Williamsburg."

"We'd never make you go back to a cruel family," Felicity assures her earnestly.

No, we wouldn't. We'd never tell on Sibyl. But I feel totally helpless. "Can we maybe . . . maybe at least help Sibyl find a good meal?" I ask Felicity.

Felicity narrows her eyes, but not in a bad way. More like she's just thinking really hard. Sibyl tucks her precious scrap of cloth back into her pocket. I wait.

Finally Felicity nods once, as if she's decided something. "Sibyl, you look like a strong girl."

Sibyl looks startled, but she nods. "Oh, aye, I'm strong. I've chopped wood and hoed corn since I was so high." She holds her hand out to suggest a six- or seven-year-old's height. A tiny glimmer of hope lights her face. "As long as I'm treated fairly, I don't mind hard

work. Do you know someone in need of a servant?"

"Better than that," Felicity says. "I can't make any promises, but come with me." She grabs Sibyl's hand. "I have an idea."

Turn to page 125.

W*hat if those men do come back?* I ask myself. *Or others like them?* I don't want to leave Felicity alone in the store. Besides, this is too much of an adventure to leave quite so fast.

I get back to picking up broken china. A single blue flower has survived on a small piece. "May I keep this?"

"Of course," Felicity says. "But . . . why?"

I'm not sure how to explain that what she sees as a bit of trash would be a precious souvenir for me. Finally I say, "It will remind me to speak up if I see something bad happening. Even if I'm scared." I check my gown for pockets and discover a slit in one of the side seams. When I poke my hand through, I find a separate pocket hanging from a strip of cloth tied around my waist. I slip the china piece inside.

We have the shop tidy by the time Mr. Merriman and Ben return. Words spill from Felicity faster and faster as she tells her father what happened. "One man threatened to start a fire!" she says indignantly.

Mr. Merriman strokes his jaw. He looks shaken. "I'm sympathetic to the Patriot cause, but 'tis a sorry day when grown men storm my shop and frighten two girls."

"We weren't frightened, Father," Felicity says. "At least . . . not much."

"I'm grateful for your quick thinking." Felicity's father puts his hand on my shoulder for a moment. It makes me feel good.

"I can't defend the way those committee men acted today, sir," Ben says. "And yet, with so many people angry at the British because of the stolen gunpowder, 'tis the perfect time for action."

I don't know how I feel about it. I mean, everybody knows the Patriots were the good guys, right? They created the United States of America. But those men shouldn't have barged in here and destroyed things.

Mr. Merriman sighs. "'Twould ruin us to throw all of the goods that came from Britain onto the trash heap. Or to let the safety committee sell them and keep the profits. I wish I could read the future."

Suddenly, I realize that I *can* read the future. I'm tempted to tell Mr. Merriman to trust that the Patriots will indeed win independence from the British. I want to say that I know for certain he's on the right path. But he'd never believe me.

"Will you talk to the men on the Committee of

Safety, Father?" Felicity asks anxiously.

"I will indeed," Mr. Merriman says. "But I must demonstrate that I'm trying to comply with the new rules."

"Where else can you purchase goods, sir?" I ask.

"Certain luxury items won't be available anywhere else," he explains. "Patriot ladies are sewing with homespun cloth instead of British silk, for example."

"But many goods are being produced in other colonies," Ben points out.

"I must act quickly," Mr. Merriman says. "First, as your friend here—" he nods at me—"was so clever to observe, goods purchased from Britain before the new rule went into place should not be affected. I will have Mistress Reed publish a notice in her newspaper, stating my intent."

"Mistress Reed?" I echo. I don't mean to interrupt—it's just that I didn't know women were allowed to run newspapers in colonial times.

"She prints the *Virginia Gazette*," Felicity says.

Mr. Merriman starts to pace, like he's building steam. "Second, I shall immediately rearrange displays to feature more local goods."

Felicity's forehead crinkles. "But Father, you already buy from most of the Williamsburg tradesmen."

"True," he agrees. "But just last week I admired pottery produced by the Pamunkeys."

Now my forehead crinkles. The Pamunkey tribe is one of the Native American groups in this area. Last fall my class took a field trip to a museum on the Pamunkey reservation, and I got to see some really old pots.

But while lots of people today admire traditional Indian crafts, I wouldn't have guessed that white people in 1775 would be interested. "Do you think . . ." I hesitate. "Do you think your customers will buy the pots?"

"Oh, without a doubt," Mr. Merriman says. "They are beautifully made."

"And having some for sale will help show the committee men that we're working hard to find new sources of goods." Ben nods. "Sir, 'tis a good plan."

"I think it best that I stay here at the store," Felicity's father says. "But visiting the print shop and purchasing pots are both urgent errands."

"We can help, Father!" Felicity exclaims eagerly. Then she glances at me.

"Of course," I agree.

"Very well," Mr. Merriman says. "Ben can accompany you girls."

"Since you're the guest, you choose where we go first," Felicity urges me. "The print shop, or to purchase pottery?"

To visit the Pamunkey Indians,
turn to page 109.

To visit Mistress Reed's print shop,
turn to page 127.

101

I appreciate the invitation to visit the Palace, but honestly, I don't want to. The British didn't treat the colonists fairly. I'm glad the Patriots stood up for what they believed in and created the United States of America. I don't want to be impressed by some fancy Palace and the people who live there.

"Thank you for including me," I say, "but I really should go look for my father."

Felicity walks with me to the front door. "I hope you visit Williamsburg again," she tells me. "I think we could become good friends."

I smile at her, trying to find proper words. "I think so, too. And I will indeed try to visit again."

After I leave the Coles' house, I start looking for a hidden spot where I can pull out the miniature painting and transport myself back to my own time. Then I hesitate. I don't have to go back right away, I realize. I feel more comfortable here now. It would be nice to have one last look around.

I wander away and end up walking past shops and tidy homes on Duke of Gloucester Street, which is the main road in Williamsburg. It's still busy, with some people heading to the Palace and others going

about their daily business. I see a farm cart loaded with cabbage and a carriage trimmed with gold paint. I smell dust and something spicy. I hear a whip crack as several men drive a bunch of oxen down the street, and violin music drifting from an open window.

The capitol building stands at the end of the street. My dad told me once that the first capitol building in America was built right here in Williamsburg. Today a British flag flies over the fancy red-brick building. But I know it won't be there for long, because grand and important things are going to happen inside that building. Patriot leaders from Virginia will help lead the American colonies to independence.

The politicians who will argue and debate inside that building are mostly rich white men, because that's the way things are in 1775. But if I've learned anything by visiting Williamsburg in Felicity's time, it's that everybody deserves to have a voice.

Maybe that's what citizenship is really all about, I think, remembering my homework assignment. Not just having the right to speak up, but actually doing it. Kids can't vote, and I want to be a veterinarian when I grow up, not a politician, but that doesn't mean I

can't look for ways to make my country a better place.

I take one last look at Williamsburg as it was in 1775. Then I pull out my necklace with the miniature painting. It's time to go home.

The End

To read this story another way and see how different choices lead to a different ending, go back to page 73.

We're helping," I tell the newcomer, and Felicity nods agreement. Ezra is growing weak, and I want to make sure he gets to a doctor. That's more important than anything else.

Without another word, the boy lopes off. "Let's go, then," Ben says.

Ben supports Ezra on one side, and Felicity and I take turns supporting him on the other side. Ezra's face is white and shines with sweat. His mouth is pressed in a tight line. I can tell his wounds hurt.

It seems to take forever to walk several blocks. Finally Ben stops. I glance up and try to make sense of where we are. "Is this a doctor's office?"

Ben gives me a strange look. "It's an apothecary shop."

I think an apothecary is more like a pharmacist than a doctor, so I'm not sure what to make of that, but it seems this is the best we can do. We help Ezra up the steps and enter a room lined with cupboards and shelves. The shelves hold blue and white crockery jars and glass bottles filled with different kinds of dried plants and seeds. Closed drawers have labels like "Crem Tartar" and "Rad Gentian" and "Rad Scammoni."

"What have we here?" the man behind the counter asks. He's short and bald and wears wire-rimmed glasses that remind me of pictures I've seen of Benjamin Franklin.

"My friend was hit with buckshot," Ben explains. "He needs his wounds checked and bandaged."

The apothecary gestures toward a door in the back wall. "Take him through to my treatment room."

We help Ezra stumble into the room behind the shop. A skeleton hangs in one corner. A bunch of instruments are laid out on a table covered with a green cloth. There's a cot near the fireplace. Ezra sinks onto the cot and closes his eyes.

The bald man bustles into the room behind us. "We'll begin with bloodletting," he decides, without even examining Ezra. He steps to the door and calls, "Phyllis? Please bring the leeches."

My stomach turns upside down. I have to get out of here, I think. Right now.

"I'll wait outside," I gasp. I grab my skirt up and run from the treatment room, through the shop, and back out the door. I feel sick to my stomach. The fresh air helps a little, but I half hope that Felicity doesn't

follow me. I've seen enough of 1775. I want to go back to my own time.

But Felicity, of course, is much too nice to ignore me. She comes outside with a worried look on her face. "Are you unwell?" she asks. "Your face is ghostly pale." She steps closer and pats my hand. "The sight of blood can make some ill, I've heard."

"Yes, that's it," I murmur. I can't say what I'm really thinking, which is that I can't stand to think about what doctoring is like in 1775.

I lean against the wall, trying to settle my nerves. After a few minutes, I'm pretty sure I won't throw up, which is a relief.

Felicity steps closer to the street and looks down the block. "Oh dear. What new trouble is this?"

Turn to page 143.

Honestly, I'm feeling a little overwhelmed by everything. I think I've had enough adventures for one day. "Felicity, I wish I could stay, but . . . I think I should go find my father."

For a moment my new friend looks as if she wants to protest. Finally she says, "I do understand."

"Will you be all right here by yourself?" I ask.

She nods. "Aye. And my father and Ben will be back any time. Farewell!" She hugs me.

I go outside and walk down the street until I find a tall hedge to hide behind. I pull out the miniature painting and, when I'm sure no one's watching, fix my gaze on the lady's eyes.

The world spins around me. Then the dizziness passes, and I'm back in my grandma's shop.

I look around the familiar room. Suddenly all the antiques she's collected seem very important. Some of the things in her shop have survived for more than two hundred years!

I go over to the shelf with the china platter on it. I'm positive it's the same pattern that Mr. Merriman had in his store. I've never given that platter any thought. Now, I wonder about it. Maybe the pretty pattern made someone smile. Maybe the notion that the china was shipped to America from Great Britain made someone else angry. Maybe the platter made some shopkeeper nervous, afraid it would bring trouble to his store.

I've always thought about the American Revolution in terms of the Declaration of Independence, and battles, and big stuff like that. Now I think that the Revolution was more complicated. The war certainly was complicated for people like Mr. Merriman, who sympathized with the Patriots but still had to feed his family. Ordinary people had to make lots of really hard choices.

I grab a clean cloth and carefully dust the pretty platter. I wish I knew the story of the person who first owned it! But I know a little of Felicity Merriman's story, and that's pretty special.

The End

To read this story another way and see how different choices lead to a different ending, go back to page 80.

It would be cool to see Pamunkey pots here—brand new! "I'd like to see the pottery," I decide.

"I doubt that any traders will be in Williamsburg today," Mr. Merriman tells Ben. "'Twould be best to go to the landing."

"I wish we could ride there," Felicity says. "I do so love to ride."

Felicity sure is lucky. Her parents didn't make her wait until she's sixteen to ride horses.

Ben smiles. "We'll take the cart, though. Then I won't have to worry about dropping pottery on the way home."

Before long we're on our way, with a horse named Old Bess pulling the cart. I like traveling like this, three across on the plank seat, even if it is jouncy. "How far are we going?" I ask.

"The Pamunkey reservation is about twenty-five miles away," Ben explains. "But we don't have to go that far. We'll visit a dock at the Pamunkey River where the Indians bring goods to sell."

As Ben steers through the crowded streets, I'm reminded of the angry Patriots, still gathering at the Governor's Palace. But soon we leave the hubbub behind.

We pass some log cabins and split-rail fences zigzagging around fields and pastures. Chickens and geese wander about the farmyards, and kids fight the weeds with big hoes. Once I see a woman guiding a plow behind a team of oxen. A small boy walks beside the oxen, sometimes tapping them with a long stick to keep them going.

We also drive through some wooded areas. Birds are singing. It's pretty and peaceful. I've probably been here before, but I don't recognize the countryside. I'm used to seeing apartment buildings and shopping centers.

We travel to a marshy river. A dock extends over the water, and there's an open area around it with lots of wheel tracks.

A white boy about Ben's age is there already, sitting on the seat of his own horse-drawn cart, whittling. He waves his hat as we approach. "Good day, Ben!" he calls.

"And to you, Roger!" Ben pulls our cart beside his friend's. "Roger is apprentice at another store," he explains.

"Did your master get a visit from the Committee of Safety today?" Roger asks.

"Aye," Ben says. "These girls were minding the store and managed to save most everything from

the over-eager committee men. But we're going to work harder to show that we're purchasing only local goods." He scans the river in both directions. "Are there no traders today?"

"Oh, they'll be along anytime now," Roger says.

Felicity and I scramble down and walk onto the dock. "Let's see how close to the edge we can walk without falling in!" Felicity says. She goes to the very edge of the dock and begins making her way around, heel-toe, heel-toe. She holds her arms out for balance as if she's walking a tightrope.

I follow Felicity. Once I almost lose my balance and have to wave my arms like windmills to stay on the dock, but I manage it. When we get all the way around, we burst out laughing, just for the fun of it.

"I'm eager to meet the traders," I tell her. "Have you come before?"

Felicity shakes her head. Before I can ask any more questions, we hear a shout. A canoe glides into view. Then another. And another.

I suddenly feel like ginger ale inside, all tingly with excitement. The Pamunkey traders are here!

As they draw closer, I see that the canoes are

dugouts—big logs split in half and then hollowed out. They are very shallow, with the sides rising just a few inches above the water. But each dugout is filled with baskets and bowls, and holds at least two people.

All the Indian traders are men. I expected them to wear buckskins or something, but they're dressed much like Ben and Roger, in knee-length cotton pants, with vests and jackets over their shirts. I've learned a little about Virginia's Native American tribes in school, but obviously there's a whole lot I don't know.

Ben and Roger walk out on the dock as the dugouts arrive. The Indian men pass their baskets up to them, then tie up their dugouts and climb up a little ladder. Now I see that most of them haven't dressed entirely like the colonists. One Pamunkey man wears a feather in his hair. One has a small silver nose ring. Another one wears earrings.

It's fascinating to see what the traders have brought. Most of it is food: baskets of dried corn, sacks of beans, glassy-eyed fish packed in damp reeds, mussels and oysters and clams. But the two young men in the third canoe have brought pottery packed in baskets among soft evergreen branches. The smallest pot could fit in

one hand, but most are bigger. They're shiny, and many have pretty designs marked on their sides. Some are tannish, and some are black. The two young men display the pottery on a blanket.

"Let's go talk to them!" I whisper to Felicity. "Oh—wait. Do you suppose they speak English?"

Felicity hesitates. "Perhaps 'twould be better if we let Ben pick out the pots."

I glance over my shoulder. Ben is talking with another Pamunkey man who appears to be selling dippers made from gourds. "Ben's busy," I say. "There's no harm in us looking at the pottery, is there?"

"No," Felicity agrees. "But you see . . . I've never actually talked to an Indian before."

Now I understand why Felicity wanted to wait for Ben. "My mother used to tell me something about meeting new people," I say. "She said it's best to think first about all the things you have in common. Then, after you get to know them a little, you can learn about some of the ways you're different."

Felicity touches my arm. "You said 'used to.' Is she dead?"

The question surprises me. Most of the kids I know

never ask that straight out. It's like they're afraid they'll upset me if they use words like "die" or "dead." Or maybe they think I've forgotten Mom, and that mentioning her would be an unhappy reminder. But I think about her every single day.

"Yes," I tell Felicity. "She got really sick, and then she died."

"I'm truly sorry," Felicity says earnestly. "I like what she told you about meeting new people."

"She had lots of smart ideas like that." I've got a little lump in my throat, but it's okay. When I remember something my mom told me, it's like a little bit of her stayed behind with me.

"Well, then." Felicity straightens her shoulders. "Let's go meet the traders."

Turn to page 158.

The six of us follow the servant down a hall. Through open doors I catch glimpses of a dining table set with silver and crystal and a ballroom with huge portraits hanging on the walls. But I can't do too much sightseeing. I'm too busy trying to copy every move Felicity makes. I can tell that she's trying hard to copy every move that Elizabeth's mother makes.

We go up a flight of stairs. Lady Dunmore is waiting in her sitting room. The ladies curtsy. Felicity and Elizabeth curtsy too, with straight backs and heads bowed and tilted a bit to one side. I curtsy so low my knees wobble. For a moment I'm afraid I'm going to fall on my butt, but I manage to straighten up again.

"Pray forgive us for calling uninvited, Lady Dunmore," Mrs. Hutchinson begins. "We came to assure you that despite the antics of some hotheads this morning, there are many in Williamsburg who continue to hold your family in great esteem and protest most vigorously to any suggestion otherwise . . ."

She goes on and on, and I kind of tune her out because there's so much to look at. Almost everything in the room is a deep, ruby red—the carpet, the walls, the upholstered chairs. Most of the furniture is pushed

against the walls, which seems weird, but it shines with polish. The red wallpaper looks like velvet, and I really want to touch it, but I figure that would be a bad idea, so I don't.

A fancy baby bed stands out against all the red, because it has white ruffles and little white curtains elegantly draped over it. The baby inside makes little cooing noises and waves her little hands as though she's trying to greet us.

Once Mrs. Hutchinson winds down, Lady Dunmore greets us. She wears an amazing fern-colored gown covered with ruffles and embroidery and satin ribbon roses. The governor's wife is a beautiful woman. But what I like best is her smile.

"The threat of hostilities earlier was unpleasant," she says, "so 'tis most kind of you to call. Will you stay for tea? We enjoyed some dancing here last night, but I'll have the servants bring out the tables."

"You are too kind," Mrs. Cole says.

"I am glad to have company today," Lady Dunmore assures her. "Although . . ." She looks past the grown-ups and smiles at Felicity, Elizabeth, and me. "My daughter Susan, who's only seven, was alarmed by

the confrontation earlier. I instructed her governess to take her outside for some fresh air. Perhaps you young ladies would prefer to play with her?"

"That is a thoughtful suggestion," Mrs. Cole says.

Honestly, I'm relieved. It was great to get a look inside the Palace, but sitting down for some fancy tea party doesn't sound like fun. In fact, trying to get through that without breaking some important rule about etiquette sounds totally stressful.

The servant takes us three girls back downstairs and out another door. There are all kinds of fancy gardens behind the Palace, and at first I don't see anyone. But the servant leads us to a gate that leads into a private grassy lawn surrounded by flower beds and a hedge. An African American man with gray hair is trimming flowers in one of the garden beds. A little boy—maybe five or six years old—is helping him.

A woman who must be the governess sits on a bench, watching a little girl roll a big wooden hoop across the grass. The girl lets it fall over when she sees us. "I bid you good day," she says politely. I can tell she's been trained to act formal, but she also sounds curious. She has freckles on her nose and friendly blue eyes.

Felicity introduces us. "We came to assure you and your mother that no one in Williamsburg wishes your family harm," she explains, and I can tell that she's trying hard to be proper, too. "I hope you weren't too frightened earlier."

"Oh, no," Susan says bravely, although worry flickers in her eyes. Then her face brightens. "I am quite glad for company, though. My brothers and sisters are all occupied. Now, what shall we do? Would you like to explore the maze? Or play quoits or other games?"

Shy Elizabeth doesn't answer. "Either would be fun," Felicity says, and glances at me. "What would you prefer?"

To explore the maze,
turn to page 138.

To play games,
turn to page 164.

I have to listen to a little voice in my head. Maybe it's me trying to make a smart decision, or maybe it's a memory of my dad talking about rules and responsibility. The situation in Williamsburg has gone from exciting to dangerous. It's time to go back to my own time.

I quickly pull Felicity aside. "May I tell you a secret? When we first met, I told you I lost my father in the crowd. Well, I didn't really lose him. I wanted to have an adventure, without getting his permission. So I just sort of . . . ran away from home."

Something in Felicity's eyes tells me that she knows exactly what I'm trying to say. "I am honored you trust me with your secret," she says. "It can be so difficult to behave properly all the time!"

I knew she'd understand. "Felicity . . ." I can't find the words to tell her how I feel about our time together. "I hope your dreams come true," I say finally, and we say good-bye.

"I hope you heal quickly," I tell Ezra. "Ben, please take good care of yourself."

I watch as they slowly walk away. Will Ben survive the American Revolution? How about Ezra, who's

already cast his fate with the army?

In my heart, I desperately hope they both survive. But I also have to face the fact that the American Revolution was a real war. Somehow it never quite seemed that way in schoolbooks. I got a tiny taste of violence this afternoon, and seeing those boys get wounded . . . and seeing that mob go crazy . . . well, it was horrible. I should never have suggested that Felicity and I join Ben and his friends on their raid. I knew all along that my dad would never have allowed it. It's hard to admit, but . . . I guess parents have good reasons for their rules.

I spot a deserted backyard and slip through the gate. There's a sheltered space between the outhouse and a huge woodpile. I crouch down where no one can see me. Then I pull out the necklace and gaze into the eyes of the woman in the miniature painting. When the twirling sensation comes, I close my eyes tight.

I don't open them again until the whirls and swirls fade away. And I'm back in my grandma's antiques shop, right where I started.

The shop is empty. It's peaceful. I walk to a case where an old pistol rests on velvet. I've never paid it any

attention before. Now I wonder who last fired it.

When I feel calmer, I climb the stairs and go into the kitchen. "Hi, Grandma."

Grandma takes her apron from its hook. "Hello! Want to help me fix supper?"

We fix spaghetti and a salad and talk about school while we eat. Then I say, "Is it all right if I call Lauren before I help with the dishes?"

"Of course, sweetie," Grandma says.

I go into the living room and make the call. "Lauren, it's me," I say. "Did you pick out a puppy?"

"We did," Lauren says. "We're going to pick her up tomorrow. She's mostly white with some black spots, so I think I'll call her Pepper."

"I can't wait to meet her," I say. "And Lauren, I hope I didn't hurt your feelings by saying I had to go home."

Instead of reassuring me, Lauren gets real quiet.

Is she honestly angry at me because I didn't go to the animal shelter with her? Maybe I need to explain things better. "My dad has strict rules. Sometimes they make me really mad, but . . . I think it's mostly because he just wants to make sure I'm safe."

"You didn't hurt my feelings," Lauren says quietly.

Over the phone it's hard to tell if she really means that, but I don't know what else to say. "So, tell me more about Pepper!" I suggest instead.

"She's eight weeks old, and a mixed breed," Lauren says. "And she's adorable."

I'm sure that Pepper is adorable, but Lauren's voice still sounds funny—not nearly as excited about the new dog as I expected. "Is something wrong?"

Lauren is quiet for so long that I think she's not going to answer. Finally she says, "You won't believe this, but sometimes I wish my parents were just a little bit strict about rules."

Is she serious? "What do you mean?" I ask her.

"Honestly, I don't think my parents care what I do or where I go." Lauren's voice is flat.

"But your mom just let you pick out a puppy," I protest. "She must care, or she wouldn't have done that for you."

"Do you want to know the real reason why my mom said I could have a dog?" Lauren asks. "As soon as we got home from the shelter, she told me she's going off on a trip with her boyfriend this weekend."

"Oh . . ."

"My dad's busy with his new family, so he said I couldn't stay over with him while she's gone. My grandpa is coming to stay with me, but all he ever wants to do is watch TV." Lauren sounds as if she's about to cry.

I don't blame her. It's as if her mom gave her a puppy as a consolation prize for being left alone so much.

I think fast. "Lauren, why don't you and your grandfather come over for supper tomorrow, and bring Pepper? I'll have to check with my dad and grandmother, but I'm sure it will be okay. I'm dying to meet Pepper, and we can hang out for a while."

"Well . . . that would be great," Lauren says, sounding brighter. "Really great."

After we hang up, I stay curled on the couch for a few minutes, thinking. Rules are tricky things. Sometimes they're totally unfair—like all the rules the British tried to force on the colonists.

But sometimes rules are fair, even if you don't like them. My dad is overprotective sometimes. But that's better than not trying to be protective at all.

I go back to the kitchen. There's no sign of my father

yet. "Grandma," I say, "how about we make a special dessert for Dad?"

She tips her head. "Sure, but . . . any particular reason?"

"Not really," I say. "I just think he deserves a treat."

The End

To read this story another way and see how different choices lead to a different ending, go back to page 68.

here are we going?" Sibyl asks. Felicity doesn't answer.

I have to hurry to catch up. Felicity charges down Duke of Gloucester Street. When we reach the Palace green, I see throngs of people, but Felicity keeps going. She doesn't stop until we reach a small shop. The yellow sign hanging over the walkway has a saw painted on it. Felicity marches right up the steps.

Inside, I recognize the man behind the counter as Master Griffith, who'd tried to talk Ezra out of quitting his apprenticeship. "I'm sorry your window frames aren't ready yet, sir," he's saying to a man who looks unhappy. "My apprentice ran off, and . . ." He gestures around the shop.

The shop is an absolute mess. The saws hanging on the walls look clean and tidy, but other tools have been heaped inside a huge open trunk. Piles of sawdust and curly wood shavings litter the floor. Pieces of wood clutter the workbenches behind the counter. It looks as if several projects got started but were never finished.

The customer glances around and sniffs as if he smells something rotten. "I shall return tomorrow. If

you have not made progress, I'll know your fine reputation is nonsense." He marches out of the shop.

Master Griffith does not look happy to see us—especially me and Felicity. "Aren't you Ezra's friends? Be gone, all of you. Ezra has caused me enough trouble."

"Sir, I'm very sorry that Ezra broke his promise to serve as your apprentice," Felicity says. "We came to solve your problem."

Master Griffith folds his arms. "And how do you intend to do that? All the young men are running off to join one of the armies."

I finally catch on to Felicity's plan, and gently push Sibyl closer to the counter. "But Sibyl here has no wish to leave Williamsburg," I say. "And she needs a job."

Master Griffith's eyebrows raise. "Take on a girl?"

❀ ***Turn to page 146.***

et's go to the print shop," I say. I'm eager to meet a woman printer from colonial days.

"I'll need a moment to compose the notice," Mr. Merriman says. "Felicity, perhaps you and your friend would enjoy a piece of rock candy while you wait." His eyes twinkle.

Felicity hands me a small chunk of something that looks like glass. I pop it in my mouth. I've never tasted rock candy before. It's very sweet, but also a bit spicy, like cinnamon. "It'th good," I mumble, because my mouth is full. Felicity giggles, and I giggle too.

It doesn't take Mr. Merriman long to compose his notice. "'William Merriman, merchant, begs leave to inform his customers, that he will sell only those British goods purchased before the sale of imported goods was declared illegal. Furthermore, he intends to fully comply with the Committee of Safety.'"

I believe "comply" means that he'll obey the committee's rules. That should calm Jack and his friends down.

Mr. Merriman hands the paper to Felicity. "Ask Mistress Reed to print this at her earliest convenience. Be sure to get a bill."

We leave the shop. "We have more than one printing press in Williamsburg," Ben tells me, "but Mr. Merriman was wise to choose the *Virginia Gazette.* Patriots wanted a newspaper that wasn't controlled by the royal governor, and asked Mistress Reed's husband to start the *Gazette*. When he died, Widow Reed became the printer."

It's a short walk to the shop. The sign hanging over the door says "Printing Office & Post Office."

"I'll wait out here," Ben says. I can tell he wants to watch everyone bustling past on the street.

Felicity and I step inside. A woman behind the counter is helping a customer, so I take a look around. Things for sale are laid out near the door—books, maps, writing paper, and even sealing wax, because people in colonial times don't have envelopes that they can lick and seal. I see a stack of the latest newspaper, too. The front page says "Virginia Gazette" in big letters across the top and "Williamsburg: Printed by Clarissa Reed."

I also see posters nailed up on the walls. They aren't pretty posters like the ones in my bedroom. These posters are mostly words, with titles like "Law" and "Proclamation." A few have headlines printed in red ink, but everything else is black and white.

This must be one of the most important places in all of Williamsburg. Nowadays people can get news from the Internet and TV and radio, not just from newspapers. But in Felicity's time, the only way to share information with a lot of people is to have it printed.

The customer must have news to share, because he's examining a poster that Mistress Reed has placed on the counter. He's a tall man, and well dressed. His red hair, which is almost the same red shade as Felicity's pretty curls, is smoothed back and tied in a ponytail.

"Will it suit, sir?" Mistress Reed asks. She wears a dark dress with a white ruffle around the neck and a white cap over her dark hair.

"Excellent, madam." He looks pleased. "This broadside is quite important, and we need fifty printed. Pray proceed with all urgency."

She smiles. "Of course, Mr. Jefferson."

My mouth slowly drops open. Mr. Jefferson? Could this possibly be—?

The man turns, sees Felicity and me, and tips his hat. "Good day," he says. And for a split second he

looks right into my eyes. Felicity politely returns his greeting, but I can't get any words out before he hurries from the shop.

Finally I find my tongue. "Was that man—was that Mr. *Thomas* Jefferson?"

Turn to page 151.

I've already traveled back in time. I don't think I want to go any farther away. "I would prefer to stay here," I tell Mrs. Merriman.

"Please, Mother," Felicity begs. "Might we stay in Williamsburg?"

Mrs. Merriman hesitates, then nods. "We shall stay—for now." She gives Felicity a stern look. "If British soldiers do arrive, we shall leave at once."

"Yes, Mother," Felicity says.

Marcus has been waiting quietly. Mrs. Merriman turns to him. "Thank you, Marcus, but I shall not require the carriage today after all."

I follow Felicity and her mother inside. Felicity and I go upstairs to her bedroom so I can change into a new dress. When I wriggle out of the one I'm wearing, I get my first good look at underwear, 1775-style. The bottom layer is a loose, lightweight, short-sleeved dress-type garment. Something made of heavy striped fabric is fastened around my chest. "No wonder I can hardly breathe!" I exclaim.

"Are your stays too tight?" Felicity murmurs sympathetically. "Mine are always too tight. I'll loosen yours."

After she adjusts the laces in back, I do feel better.

The stays make me want to stand up straight, but they aren't uncomfortable anymore. And her spare dress is a perfect fit. "I look almost as stylish as you," I tell Felicity. "Your necklace is lovely."

She fingers the reddish-orange beads. "Coral is for good luck. What does your necklace look like?"

I pull the chain free of my kerchief and hold the miniature away from me so Felicity can see it—and so I don't mistakenly transport myself back to modern times.

"Oh, how pretty," she says, leaning close. "Is that your mother?"

It's not, of course, but I nod.

Felicity's eyes grow sad. "Would you like to see my miniature?"

I nod again. She opens a wooden box and removes a small string of coral beads and a tiny painting in an oval frame. When I see the portrait, I feel as if someone is squeezing my heart. The miniature shows a very young girl. I know from Felicity's expression that this child is no longer living. "Who—who is this?" I ask.

"Her name was Charity," Felicity says. "We were dear friends when we were little. She caught a terrible fever and died."

When my mom died, I was very angry because I thought she was too young to pass away. But Charity was just a small child. "I'm sorry."

"Charity's mother gave me her coral beads." Felicity touches the necklace gently. "Sometimes I wear them to remember my friend."

We hear Mrs. Merriman calling. Felicity puts her treasures away, and I tuck my miniature painting back beneath my kerchief. Then we go downstairs and find the table set. My stomach growls at the sight. I guess I'm hungry!

Nan joins us, and we sit at the table. Felicity carefully pours hot chocolate from a silver pot into china teacups, one for each of us. She makes every move look graceful. I'm so busy watching her that I'm startled when she turns to me and says, "Would you like some cakes?"

"Well, I'd like a piece of cake," I say. Then I see that the plate she's passing is piled with cookies. "Oh, I thought—that is—yes, please," I stammer. I take two cookies that look like gingersnaps.

After we've eaten, Nan goes upstairs to tend William. Mrs. Merriman leads us into the parlor. "Perhaps you

older girls would enjoy some music?" she suggests.

"I'd rather go outside and play," Felicity whispers to me.

I would rather do just about anything than listen to music. Music is something special that my mom and I shared. She taught me to play guitar. We always sang in the car, or when we did dishes.

Mrs. Merriman sits down at a little piano-type instrument and plays a melody while Felicity and I try to sit still. When she finishes, we clap politely.

"Thank you," Mrs. Merriman says. "But Felicity, I could hardly concentrate with you fidgeting so! Let's sing together, shall we?"

She plays another song, and she and Felicity sing. I don't know the words, but I'm getting such a lump in my throat that I wouldn't be able to join in anyway.

After playing the last chord, Mrs. Merriman turns to me. "Do you like music, my dear?"

"I . . . yes, ma'am, I do." I swallow hard. "My mother and I used to sing together. And she taught me how to play the guitar."

"You play the guitar?" Felicity gasps. "Truly? Miss Manderly, my teacher, says I may take lessons when

I'm twelve. But I already have a guitar." She jumps up and carefully fetches a guitar from a high shelf. "This belonged to my grandmother." She cradles the guitar, then offers it to me. "Will you play for us?"

"Oh no, I—I couldn't." I haven't touched my own guitar since Mom died.

Felicity clasps her hands together. "Please?"

"Your guest may not wish to play," Mrs. Merriman says. Then she looks at me. "But we would be honored to hear a melody, child."

I find myself reaching for the guitar. It's very different from any guitar I've ever seen before—smaller, and curvy, with a rounded back. But the strings feel familiar beneath my fingers. I tune the guitar. Then I close my eyes and play a song. When I finish, Felicity applauds.

"That was lovely," Mrs. Merriman says softly. "And took some courage, I suspect."

Courage? I think with surprise. But . . . maybe it does take a little courage to face even simple things after someone you love dies. Playing Felicity's guitar made my heart hurt. But it also made me feel closer to Mom than I have for a long time.

Suddenly all I want to do is go home. I want to get my guitar out from under my bed and play Mom's favorite songs. I also want to unpack the old family photos and videos. I want to tell my dad that hiding them doesn't protect us from grief—it makes our grief worse. Besides, we're super lucky to have lots of pictures and videos of Mom, and not just one tiny painting.

"Thank you for encouraging me to play." I hand the guitar back to Felicity. "I think I should change back into my own dress now and go look for my father."

Felicity's mother nods. "I'll fetch your gown. I mended the tear and cleaned off the worst of the dirt."

Upstairs, I wriggle into the dress. When my head pops through, I see Felicity holding the little string of coral beads that once belonged to her friend Charity.

"I'd like you to have these," Felicity says.

My eyes go wide. "Oh, I couldn't! They help you remember your friend!"

"I have the miniature to remind me of Charity," Felicity says. "I want you to have something to remind you of me."

The beads feel warm and smooth in my hand. "I will treasure this," I say. "And Felicity? I promise, I will never forget you."

The End

To read this story another way and see how different choices lead to a different ending, go back to page 64.

et's explore the maze!" I suggest. I went through a corn maze once, and it was a blast.

Susan takes us through a gate that leads into the maze. This maze isn't made of cornstalks but of smoothly sheared hedges, which are planted to form narrow walkways. The hedges are thick and much taller than me.

"There are lots of paths inside, with many turns and dead ends," Susan tells us. "Why don't we each go our own way and see who can reach the center first?"

The rest of us agree, although I figure that since Susan lives at the Palace, and has surely been through the maze many times, she probably knows how to get to the center quickly. Still, I like puzzles, and maybe I can beat Felicity and Elizabeth.

We walk into the maze and go in different directions. It's cool and shady in here, and birds are chirping. Sometimes the carefully clipped branches brush against my arms. I slow down because the last thing I want to do is damage the gown Elizabeth's mother loaned me. I can hear the other girls giggling or calling to one another, coming closer and fading away, but I can't see them. Then—"I'm in the center!" Susan calls.

That didn't take long! Just as I expected. Oh, well. I turn and walk down a long corridor that seems to lead toward the maze's center, but I hit a dead end. I retrace my steps, make another choice, and reach another dead end. I feel as if I'm farther from the center than ever.

One of my stockings is falling down, and I use this private moment to stop and get it tied back into place. Suddenly I hear a whisper of conversation—but the voice is not one of my friends; it's a man's voice! "Dunmore promised peace to our people if the four of us stay here in Williamsburg," the man mutters.

"We aren't guests," another man scoffs. "We are hostages. If the Shawnee fight the colonists who continue to steal our lands on the frontier, Dunmore will make us pay."

The men are outside the maze, just on the other side of the hedge. I've gone as still as a stump, crouched down, and straining to hear without giving myself away. These must be the Shawnee men Felicity told me about.

"I do not believe Dunmore will stay in the city if his family continues to be threatened," the first man says. "What will happen to us then?"

One of his companions says angrily, "We should

leave this place and go back to the Shawnee. Now."

"I say we wait and see what happens," another man protests. "If Dunmore believes we broke our promise to stay, our people could suffer."

I spot a tiny opening in the hedge and slowly lean close, trying really hard not to make any noise. Through the branches I get a look at the Indian men, and my breath catches in my throat. They are wearing leather leggings and moccasins, with no shirts. The man closest to me has shaved most of his head, leaving a long black ponytail in back. His scalp and forehead are stained red with some kind of paint or dye, and his face is decorated with dark lines and triangles. He wears a silver ring in his nose and big rings inside his earlobes that have stretched out the skin and make his ears long. He looks intense.

"I don't believe the Patriots will back down," he says urgently. "We should form an alliance with the Long Knives and help them drive the British back to England—"

"Our agreement is with Dunmore, not with the Long Knives . . ." Their voices fade as they walk away.

"Long Knives" must mean the colonists. We learned

in school that the Shawnee people sometimes fought the pioneer colonists who wanted to move west and take their land. It sounds as if these men are trying to figure out whether they should join the Patriots, stay loyal to the British, or go home to their own village. They realize that war is coming, and they're trying to guess what will be best for their people in the long run.

Before I came back to 1775, when I thought of the Revolutionary War, I thought about the colonists fighting the British, and I assumed the colonists were all on the same side, against the British. But I realize now that the war was a lot more complicated than that. There were Patriots and Loyalists and people who just wanted to be left alone. There were enslaved people and free black people. There were Cherokee people and Shawnee people and many other Native Americans. And all of them had to make life-and-death decisions about their future without knowing what would happen next.

It occurs to me that the Indians must feel sort of as if they're wandering in a maze—trying to avoid dead ends, hoping to find a peaceful path forward.

I wish I had a notebook and pen, because my time

here is giving me a lot of good ideas for the persuasive essay about citizenship I'm supposed to write.

Suddenly I hear Felicity calling my name. "Are you lost? The rest of us have reached the center!"

"I'll find you!" I call back. My homework can wait, because I know I won't forget one minute of my adventure in 1775.

The End

To read this story another way and see how different choices lead to a different ending, go back to page 118.

I follow her gaze. There's some new commotion in the next block. A small group of shouting men—and some women—has gathered around a tall pole. "Why is that skinny tree trunk there?" I ask. I haven't seen anything like it.

"'Tis our Liberty Pole," Felicity says. "Are you feeling better? I'd like to go see what's happening."

Hanging around the apothecary shop isn't going to make me feel better, that's for sure. "Let's go," I tell Felicity. She takes off down the street, and I hurry after her.

As we approach the crowd, I see a small keg and a white sack hanging from a crosspiece nailed at the top of the pole.

"What is this Liberty Pole all about?" I ask.

"Patriots erected it to send a message to Loyalist men," Felicity explains. "The keg represents tar, and the sack is filled with feathers." She hesitates, chewing her bottom lip. "I don't think the Patriots would ever *really* tar and feather a Loyalist, though. 'Tis just meant to make them think."

As we walk closer, I hear jeering voices. "Still loyal to the British king, are you?" a man taunts.

"We don't need your kind in Williamsburg!" a woman shrieks. She raises her arm and throws an egg toward the pole.

When we wriggle close, I'm horrified to see that the person being tormented is not a man, but a boy—no older than eleven or twelve. The Patriots have backed the boy against the Liberty Pole and tied his hands behind it.

Felicity gasps. "Why, 'tis Joseph Miller!" she says. "His father's a tutor."

Joseph wears a fine coat, but it's stained with the garbage people have thrown at him. A man with a scar on one cheek snatches the brown wig from Joseph's head and tosses it into the street. Joseph's head is covered with an uneven stubble of hair, and the man hoots with laughter.

"Oh, I can't stand this!" I hiss to Felicity. "I don't want to watch." It's almost worse than the apothecary shop.

"Poor lad," Felicity murmurs. "Brave, though."

She's right. Joseph's eyes are filled with tears, but his head is held high. He stands still, even as these mean grown-ups shove him and throw spoiled food at him.

Felicity's hands clench into fists. "We must help him."

I want to help Joseph. I really do. But what can two girls do?

Turn to page 167.

Girls can do more than sew and bake," Felicity tells him. "'Tis not unheard of for a girl to learn such a trade as yours."

"No, but most often 'tis a case of her father owning the shop." He frowns. But it's a thoughtful frown, not an angry one.

At first Sibyl seemed totally blown away by Felicity's suggestion, but now she gestures toward the messy room. "Sir, I can be of service to you. I am strong, and a hard worker. I can cipher too, so long as the numbers aren't too big. Treat me fairly and I'll give you no cause for complaint."

Master Griffith rubs his chin, staring at her.

"What exactly does a joiner do?" I ask, trying to give him time to come around to our way of thinking.

He grabs something from one of the workbenches and puts it on the counter. Two narrow pieces of wood have been put together to make two sides of a square. "I shaped the wood and used a peg to join the pieces together, see?" he asks. He seems to forget his worry for a moment, and I can tell he loves to show people his work.

"Is this part of a window frame?" I ask.

"Indeed." He nods. "Think of it this way: A carpenter builds a house, a joiner finishes it, and a cabinet maker furnishes it."

"Now I understand," I tell him. "Thank you for explaining it."

Master Griffith looks back to Sibyl. "There's nothing about the work itself that a girl your size couldn't handle. But tell me this: Do you actually wish to learn the joiners' trade?"

She catches her breath. Her eyes get a glassy look as if she's trying not to cry. "Sir, the chance to learn from you would be more than I've ever dared dream. If you'll give me a chance to prove myself, I'll gladly pledge the next seven years to your service."

I hold my breath. I think Felicity is holding her breath, too. An apprenticeship would mean more than Sibyl getting food and shelter. Learning a trade would mean she'd have a career.

Another customer steps into the shop. "Master Griffith? I'm having a new house built in town. I need door frames, and window frames, and two mantels to mount over the fireplaces."

"Done," the master joiner tells Sibyl in a low voice.

"You can start by sweeping up." Then he beckons the customer over to the counter. "Yes, sir. You've come to the right place."

Felicity and Sibyl and I retreat to one corner. I want to squeal and jump up and down, but that's probably not a good idea, so I do my best to stuff my happiness down inside.

Sibyl's happiness leaks out in the tears sliding down her cheeks. "I don't know how to thank you," she whispers, swiping at her eyes.

"There's no need," Felicity assures her. "I hope everything goes well."

"Oh, it will." Sibyl's voice is full of determination. She hugs us both. Then she slips behind the counter, grabs the broom propped in one corner, and gets to work.

Felicity and I go back outside. "That idea was brilliant," I tell her. "You did something amazing today."

She sighs. "It's hard to imagine Sibyl's mother abandoning her baby at the foundling home."

I think about my own mom. She went through three rounds of chemotherapy treatment, trying to stay with me and Dad for as long as she could. All we really

know about Sibyl's mom is that she left that scrap of her dress behind with her baby. "I think Sibyl's mother didn't really abandon her," I say slowly. "She wanted to come back for Sibyl one day. And by leaving her baby at the foundling home, she knew that if she couldn't return for her, Sibyl would at least learn some skills so she could make a living." It wasn't much. I felt certain that leaving her baby must have been an enormous sacrifice for Sibyl's mom, one that broke her heart, all because she wanted the best for her baby in a time and place that didn't give her any other options.

"I think Sibyl will do well here," Felicity says.

"I do too." I smile. "And now that Sibyl's taken care of, I think I should go look for my father." I only have one parent left, and suddenly I really, really want to see him.

"Of course. And if you visit again, we can stop by to see Sibyl," Felicity suggests. "Just to see how she's faring."

"I'd like that," I say. "And I'd really like to see you again, too."

Felicity grins, then catches her breath. "I know!" She pulls off her cap and removes a pretty purple

ribbon decorating it. "I can't offer a piece of my dress. My mother would be quite cross! But I offer this ribbon as a token of our friendship."

I quickly pull off my cap so I can offer a ribbon as exchange. "Remember me," I say. "I do hope to come back one day."

Felicity tucks my gift into her pocket. Instead of doing that, I twine her ribbon through my fingers. I want to make sure it gets back to my own time with me.

After we say good-bye, I slip around the joiner's shop and crouch down behind the big well in the backyard. When I stare at the lady's face in the miniature painting, I have just a moment to wonder whether she was a mom. There's something in her eyes that makes me believe she was, and that she loved her kids a whole lot. Just like my mom loved me, and just like I think Sibyl's mom loved her.

Then the dizziness comes, and I have to shut my eyes.

Turn to page 172.

Yes, indeed it is," Mistress Reed says. "I often work for Mr. Jefferson. Last year, when he wrote the first document to publicly argue for overthrowing British rule, I had the honor of publishing it."

I don't understand why Felicity isn't jumping up and down with excitement. I want to grab her hands and say, "That was *Thomas Jefferson*! The man who wrote the *Declaration of Independence*! And later became *president!*"

But just in time, I remember that I'm visiting in *1775*—the year *before* Thomas Jefferson wrote the Declaration of Independence. Mistress Reed and Felicity have never even heard of the famous document, which announced to the world the Patriots' plan to form a new nation in 1776.

Felicity leans close. "Are you quite well?" she asks. "Your cheeks have gone rosy."

"I'm fine," I whisper back. "Just—just a bit warm."

Felicity hands Mistress Reed the note. "Mistress Reed, my father wishes to publish a notice in the *Virginia Gazette* at your earliest convenience. I'm to take the bill."

Mistress Reed reads the notice and looks pleased. "Of course, Miss Merriman. Your father's decision

is sure to inspire other merchants."

While she writes up a bill for Felicity, I wander away. I'm still trembling because I met Thomas Jefferson.

I'm also curious about the shop. The printing press sits behind the counter. Strange tools hang on the walls. Pages of newsprint dangle from strings criss-crossed overhead like clotheslines so the ink can dry. Both of the men working have rolled up their sleeves and wear leather aprons to protect their clothes.

One sits in front of a cabinet with lots of small compartments. His hands fly back and forth, snatching little pieces of metal and arranging them in a wooden frame. I probably shouldn't interrupt him, but when he gives me a friendly glance, I take a chance. "What are you doing?" I ask.

"Why, setting type." He holds up one of the metal pieces for my inspection. It has a tiny letter *O* on one end. I realize that he's grabbing letters and arranging them into words, and the words into sentences. It must take hours to set one whole page of type.

The other man is working at the press. The main part of the press is flat, like a table. Fixed on the press is a frame holding enough tiny pieces of type to create an

entire newspaper page. The man dabs at the type with what looks like a leather ball that's partly stained black. "Are you putting on the ink?" I ask.

"Aye." His tone is polite, but he doesn't pause. "'Tis a mixture of varnish and lampblack."

I'll never take writing on a computer for granted again!

A piece of blank paper is in another frame that sits straight up and down and is attached to the table part with hinges. The man grabs a handle and pulls that frame down so the blank paper is pressed hard against the inky type. When he lifts the handle again, I see a perfectly printed sheet of newspaper.

Mistress Reed and Felicity are finished. As Felicity tucks the bill away in her pocket, I look at Mistress Reed. "Pardon me, ma'am, but may I ask a question? Do you like running the print shop?"

"Do I *like* it?" Mistress Reed looks startled, as if she'd never thought about that. "'Twas a matter of necessity. When death snatched my husband, and my children were hungry, I prayed that God might make me equal to the task of running the shop."

I can hardly imagine how hard it must have been

to take over the business when her husband died. "Did men in Williamsburg accept you?"

"I believe so, for the most part." Mistress Reed tips her head thoughtfully. "I did not miss printing even a single edition of the *Gazette*. Virginia officials allowed me to inherit my husband's official position as public printer. I believe I have earned their trust. I'm proud to provide a voice for the Patriot cause."

"That is something to be proud of," I agree. "But . . . could you have become a printer if your husband hadn't died?" This might be something to talk about this summer when I'm a junior interpreter, so I really want to understand.

Mistress Reed loses the faraway look and folds her arms. "No indeed," she says briskly. "But it does please me. As each issue declares, I will consider news provided by all parties, but I print only what I choose."

As Felicity and I leave the shop, my thoughts are tumbling.

"I think I must say good-bye now," I tell Felicity. I feel ready to burst with all the new things I've seen and learned. I don't think I should try to cram in any more.

"Yes, 'tis best that you find your father," she agrees.

"I wish I could accompany you, but my father is waiting for me. Thank you for your help."

"It was an adventure!" I tell her, and say good-bye to her and Ben.

Felicity walks away with a bounce in her step. I know that her father is facing enormous challenges, but I believe in my heart that the Merrimans will come through the Revolutionary War just fine.

I find a hidden spot behind the shop. I reach into my pocket and grab the bit of broken china I saved. With my other hand I pull out the miniature painting hung around my neck. Quick as a flash, I'm back in my grandmother's shop.

I can hear her working in the kitchen. I want to charge upstairs and yell, Grandma, guess what? I met Thomas Jefferson!

But of course I can't say that. She'd think I was nuts. In fact, I'm doubly relieved when I realize the tiny piece of china traveled through time with me. It's a cool souvenir, and it will remind me that I didn't dream the whole adventure!

I'll never forget meeting Felicity or going to the print shop. I mean, Clarissa Reed was just as much of a Patriot

as Thomas Jefferson. She took risks by publishing rebellious ideas on broadsides and in her newspaper. After all, she had no way of knowing whether the Patriots would win independence—and if the British had won, they would have considered her a traitor. What would have happened to her and her children then?

Mistress Reed was very brave. Way back in 1775, she proved that women could take on a man's job and do it well. My teacher would call her a trailblazer.

I go upstairs and find my grandma in the kitchen. "Can I ask a question?" Grandma smiles and nods as she ties on her apron. I slide into my chair at the table. "Was it hard to start your antiques shop?"

"In some ways it was," Grandma admits. "When I was growing up, there weren't many women who ran stores, so I wasn't confident I could do it. I loved antiques, but I worried about handling the business part.

I nod. "But you didn't let your worries stop you."

"Nope," Grandma agrees cheerfully. "It was scary to buy this building and invest in enough antiques to fill the shop. I've made lots of mistakes along the way. But I've had the business for many years now."

She starts to fill a pot with water. A box of

spaghetti is sitting on the counter.

"I'm proud of you, Grandma." It's never occurred to me to say it before. But I am.

"You know what?" She puts the pot on the stove. "I'm proud of me, too. And the next time you tackle something that's a little scary, I'll be just as proud of you."

I get up and start setting the table. I've wanted to be a veterinarian forever. When I think about helping animals, I'm certain that it's what I want. When I think about going to college one day and taking lots of hard classes to learn how to help animals . . . well, sometimes that stresses me out.

I'll just have to remember how Felicity, and Clarissa Reed, and my grandma faced their challenges. I'm pretty sure that if I do that, I'll be just fine, too.

The End

To read this story another way and see how different choices lead to a different ending, go back to page 100.

We walk over to the two Pamunkey pottery sellers. One has long black hair. He wears pants that are a pinkish color, and a blue vest, and a brightly patterned kerchief around his neck. The other has shorter hair and is dressed more simply in white pants and a big shirt that hangs halfway down to his knees and a wide straw hat. He's sitting on the ground.

The one with long hair nods politely. He looks about Ben's age, maybe a year or so older. "Do you young ladies wish to purchase a pot?"

"Oh!" The word just pops out of my mouth. The trader looks startled, and I feel my cheeks get warm. "I'm sorry. It's just that—I wasn't sure whether you spoke English." *Especially such proper English,* I think.

"I speak several languages," he says.

Well, that makes me feel like an even bigger idiot.

"My name is Robert," he adds. "And this is my brother Alden."

Alden nods, but he doesn't look up. Maybe I insulted him by suggesting that he and his brother don't speak my language.

Before I can speak again, I hear Robert catch his breath. "What a fine animal," he says softly.

I follow his gaze and see a rider approaching. He has big saddlebags, so he must be coming to buy something. The man is riding a gorgeous horse. It's mostly black, with four white socks and a white blaze down its nose. The horse trots briskly and holds its head high as if he knows we're admiring him.

Felicity, who'd been hanging back, steps closer and gives Robert a warm smile. "Do you like horses? I love horses."

"I do as well," Robert says. "And one day I shall own such a beautiful animal."

"That's my dream, too," Felicity confesses.

Mom, I say silently, *you were one smart lady.*

Now Felicity is comfortable asking other questions. "Did you and your brother attend the Brafferton School?"

Robert tears his gaze from the horse. "We did."

Alden's expression is hard. He reaches into a pocket and pulls out a stone and what looks like a piece of green glass and begins striking the stone against the glass.

I have no idea what he's doing, but I decide not to ask. "Can you tell me about your pots?" I ask Robert

instead.

"Our mother made them," he explains. "We dig the clay from the riverbank on our reservation and help her prepare it, but she shapes the pots."

"I like all the different kinds of pots," Felicity says.

"Our mother knows many styles," Robert says proudly. "Some are traditional to my people. Some are what you newcomers prefer."

Now Ben joins us. He gives Robert and Alden a friendly greeting before turning to Felicity. "Your father gave me leave to purchase half a dozen pots. Does something strike your fancy?"

Soon Ben and Felicity have picked out bowls and storage containers for the store. Each pot is different, and I think they've made good choices. Ben pays for the pots and begins carrying them to the cart.

"Please tell your mother her pots are beautiful," I say. "And—I hope I didn't insult you by thinking that you might not speak English. You must be very smart."

"How fortunate that you were able to learn to read and write," Felicity adds.

Alden's hands go still, and he looks up. "We have been trained to act like good English people," he says

flatly. "We were instructed to teach our families what you whites want us to know. I'm glad, because knowing how to read and write English will help us understand your laws. Now we can protect our tribe's rights."

"Alden," Robert says quietly. That's all, but Alden nods. He starts striking the piece of glass again. I see now that he's creating an arrowhead shape.

Which is pretty cool. He's using an old, old skill with a new material to make something special. "You're good traders," I say, nodding at the glass arrowhead.

Robert smiles. "Pamunkey people were trading for all sorts of goods long before white people arrived here. We have always adopted new things that we find useful."

Felicity and I say good-bye and walk back toward the cart. "Is the Brafferton a school just for Indian kids?" I ask her.

"Just for Indian boys," she corrects me. "So they can be educated."

I learned in school that many Indian people have lost their own language over the years. That makes me sad. Of course, there are many sad things about

the history between white people and Indians. "Does anyone in Williamsburg send their sons to be educated about things the Pamunkey people know?" I ask.

Felicity looks astonished. "Of course not!" After a few moments, her surprise fades, and she looks thoughtful. "Although . . . it would be interesting, wouldn't it?" She tips her head to one side. "I don't know why I never thought about that before."

We've reached the cart, and Ben hears that last bit. "We won't be visiting the reservation today," he reminds her. "Your father has much for us to do!" He nestles the last pot in a heavy cotton sack filled with straw, so it won't break as we jounce along over the rutted road to Williamsburg. "Shall we go?"

He gives me a hand so I can climb to the seat, and soon we're driving back toward the city. We don't talk about the Indian school anymore. But I'm glad to know that Pamunkey people still live near Williamsburg in my time. The ones I've met live modern lives, just like anybody else, but they respect their heritage and traditions. In fact, a few are interpreters at Colonial Williamsburg.

I know that things are different in Felicity's time,

and the colonists think they're doing something good by encouraging the Indian people to act like them. But maybe, in a tiny way, I helped Felicity think about the situation differently. I've sure learned a lot from her, so it's good to think that I might have taught her something, too.

For no particular reason, Felicity bumps me with her shoulder. I bump her back. We both smile as if we've shared something special.

And I think we have.

The End

To read this story another way and see how different choices lead to a different ending, go back to page 21.

choose to play games. I want to find out what quoits are!

Susan leads us to a corner of the lawn where a stake has been pounded into the ground. Half a dozen rings made from rope lie on the grass nearby. "We will take turns trying to toss the rings over the stake," she explains. "After each round, we take a step farther away from the stake and try again. I'll show you."

She picks up the rope rings, puts a stick on the ground a short distance from the stake, and stands behind it.

"Are we supposed to let Susan win?" Elizabeth whispers. "She is the governor's daughter."

"She's younger than the rest of us, too," Felicity whispers back.

Susan gets four of her six rings looped around the stake. Then Felicity takes a turn. She gets two out of six. Neither Elizabeth nor I get any rings over the stake. I'm not sure whether I missed out of nervousness about playing with a royal governor's daughter or whether I'm just horrible at this game.

We all stand looking at one another. Susan thinks for a moment, then brightens. "I know! I have a new

kite," she says. "I haven't tried it yet, but there is a good breeze today. Shall I get it?"

"That sounds pleasant, Miss Susan," Felicity says politely.

Susan fetches her kite. It's made of white silk painted with a bright yellow sun, a blue moon, and two red stars. She puts the kite on the grass and unwinds some string.

I back up to give her room, moving closer to the flower bed. The little boy has stopped gardening to watch our games.

"Back to work, Ruben," the elderly man says gently. "You need to make yourself useful, and gardening is a good skill." That's probably great advice, but I can tell from Ruben's face that he would much rather be playing than learning a useful skill.

Susan runs across the lawn. She holds the string high, but the kite just bumps across the grass.

"This will never work," Felicity mutters. She raises her voice and calls, "Miss Susan, may I help? You'll have more luck if I hold the kite up while you handle the string."

Felicity and Susan try again. Felicity waits for just

the right moment and tosses the kite into the air. Susan trots backward, keeping an eye on the kite. "Watch out!" I call as Susan nears a patch of tulips.

"I'll help you!" Elizabeth offers, and runs to join in. The kite spirals sideways a few times as if it isn't sure it wants to fly today. Finally it takes a nosedive toward the ground near the flower bed.

Ruben jumps up and grabs the kite right before it crashes. "I got it!" he calls triumphantly.

The elderly man looks troubled. I catch my breath. Is Ruben going to get in trouble?

Turn to page 174.

Felicity doesn't stop to wonder what two girls can do. She just marches right up to Joseph and faces the crowd. "Stop this at once!" she cries.

"Isn't that the Merriman girl?" someone asks.

"I *am* the Merriman girl," Felicity says. "And you know my father sympathizes with the Patriot cause. But—"

"Go home, girl!" the scarred man shouts. "If you're a Patriot, as you say, you should know better than to interfere."

I'm close enough to hear Joseph mutter, "Thank you, miss, but please—be on your way before they turn on you."

Well, that does it for me. I'm scared. I'm also so angry that I feel as if water is boiling inside.

I step forward and join Felicity and Joseph. "I am a Patriot too," I declare to the crowd, "but watching you makes me feel ashamed. I thought Patriots were good people! I thought Patriots believe in justice and freedom! Why are you treating Joseph this way?"

"His father hasn't signed a promise to support our cause," one of the men says. He's defiant, but at least he's stopped shouting. "We must send a clear message—"

"Mr. Griggs," Felicity calls in a haughty voice, "I believe you have not paid your bill at my father's store for at least two months past. Should my family tie you to a pole and throw rotten cabbages to send *you* a clear message?"

"Aye, Griggs," a woman with bad teeth jeers. "She's called you out, she has!"

People laugh. Mr. Griggs glares at Felicity, but he can't find anything to say.

Another man steps close, pulls a knife from a sheath at his belt, and uses it to slice the ropes binding Joseph's hands. "There, lad," he says gruffly. "No harm done."

I glare at the man with the knife, because I'm pretty sure that harm has been done. But when Felicity grabs one of Joseph's hands and tows him away, I'm smart enough to get out of there, too.

Joseph snatches his wig from the street, and we walk away from the Liberty Pole as fast as we can—one block, two blocks. Finally we stop, almost breathless. "Are you all right?" Felicity asks Joseph.

Joseph looks as if he just crawled from a compost pile in somebody's garden, and his shaved head gives him a sickly appearance, but he still stands tall. "I am," he says,

and his voice only shakes a tiny bit. "Thanks to you."

"I'm so sorry you were treated that way," I say. "I never thought Patriots would do such a thing."

"I will be on my way home now," he says. "But I remain in your debt."

Felicity and I watch Joseph hurry away. I still have a sick feeling in the pit of my stomach, but it doesn't have anything to do with leeches now.

"I always think of the Patriots as the good guys," I murmur. "But those men at the Magazine were out of control. And for people who call themselves Patriots to treat a boy like that when they're really angry at his father . . ."

"'Tis a disgrace," Felicity agrees quietly. We're both silent for a long moment. I'm feeling disappointed. My teacher called Patriots "the fathers of our country," and I can't stand to think of those cruel men as fathers of anything.

Suddenly here comes Mr. Griggs, trotting down the street like he's in a big hurry. His face is red. Nobody's chasing him, but there are some new stains on his shirt. Something glistens on his hat—it looks like an egg or two!

Felicity and I burst out laughing. "Look at him go!" she gasps.

"I don't think he'll pick on anybody else anytime soon," I add. "Serves him right!"

We laugh and laugh, and it makes me feel a bit better. Finally Felicity says, "We can't let a few braggarts and cowards change the way we feel about independence. That's what's important."

"Yes it is," I agree. "But . . . Felicity? I must go find my father now. He—he will want to know that I am safe."

"I've never seen such trouble in Williamsburg before," she says, "so I do understand." For a moment she looks worried. Then she straightens her shoulders. "Now, I best go back to the apothecary and see if Ben and Ezra need me."

I have a lot to think about as I walk away. I guess I have to stop believing in good guys and bad guys. I'm really sorry I saw Patriots acting so badly. But I've seen some good things today, too. I'd always assumed that girls didn't get to do much in colonial times. But while it's true that Felicity doesn't have nearly as many opportunities as most girls do in my time, she finds lots of ways to make a difference.

I'm really starting to look forward to being a junior interpreter at Colonial Williamsburg this summer. I have more to talk about than I ever could have imagined.

The End

To read this story another way and see how different choices lead to a different ending, go back to page 86.

The whole world whirls and twirls. Finally it slows down again. When I open my eyes, I'm back in my grandmother's shop.

I help Grandma make dinner, and we eat, and clean up . . . and all the while I'm waiting for Dad to come home.

"Gracious! You're fidgety as a June bug this evening!" Grandma says finally. She's not really scolding. More curious.

Before I can even try to explain, I hear a door slam below. Then Dad's footsteps start coming up the stairs.

I run to meet him, and wrap my arms around him in a big hug.

"What's all this?" Dad asks, hugging me back.

I can never explain what happened to me this afternoon. I can't even find the words to apologize to him for getting so mad at him and his rules. I was stupid to get upset about that. All I know right now is that my dad will never, ever leave me in a foundling home. He will never sign a contract that says I have to go work for strangers for years on end.

"Hey, Pumpkin." Dad sounds concerned now. "Is everything okay?"

"Yes." I nod, his shirt smooth against my cheek. "Everything is great."

The End

To read this story another way and see how different choices lead to a different ending, go back to page 41.

But instead of scolding Ruben for leaving his duties, Susan shouts, "Oh, thank you! Now, hold the kite up as high as you can!"

Susan and Ruben try one more time—and suddenly the kite takes off, soaring higher and higher into the sky.

Felicity claps her hands, calling, "Let out more string!"

"'Tis flying!" Susan cries. She has a big smile on her face.

"Come over this way!" Elizabeth shouts. Her warning keeps Susan from running smack into a tree.

Ruben grins as he watches the kite go higher still. Felicity and I clap and cheer, and Elizabeth bursts out laughing with delight.

When I'm a junior interpreter this summer, I will remember this moment. My main jobs will be to demonstrate colonial chores to modern kids and to talk about how the Revolutionary War would have changed their lives. But now I know that I also want to remind visitors that most of all, kids are just kids. It doesn't matter if they're Patriots or Loyalists, or whether they lived back in 1775 or are growing up in

modern times—*all* kids love to have fun.

The kite is still climbing. "I don't know if I can hold it!" Susan shrieks.

"Hang on!" I call, and run to help.

The End

To read this story another way and see how different choices lead to a different ending, go back to page 21.

ABOUT Felicity's Time

Travelers visiting Williamsburg in Felicity's time met many different kinds of people. The area's original residents included Indians of several tribes, each with their own culture and identity. As English colonists settled Virginia, Indians tried to protect their land and traditions. Tribal leaders struggled to make wise choices for their people in a time of great change.

By 1775, Williamsburg's population included wealthy landowners, middle-class families like the Merrimans who owned small businesses, and poor laborers. Young people like Ben who weren't wealthy often became apprentices to learn a trade, such as shopkeeping or glassblowing. Others became indentured servants by agreeing to work without pay for a certain number of years in exchange for passage to America or as payment for a crime. Although most girls were indentured as maids and household workers, some were indentured to learn a trade, such as dressmaking.

The wives and daughters of silversmiths, shoemakers, and other skilled craftsmen often helped in the family business. One woman, Clementina Rind, was able to take charge of her husband's printing shop after he died. She published the *Virginia Gazette* and writings by Thomas Jefferson.

Slightly more than half of the Virginians were African American. A few free blacks earned their living as workers or skilled craftspeople. Most black people were enslaved workers who labored on tobacco plantations, although some slaves worked in towns. By Felicity's time, slavery had become the foundation of Virginia's great wealth.

On plantations, the cabins in the slave quarter were small and rough. Still, for field workers working in brutal conditions, the quarter was a place of refuge. People tended gardens and raised chickens. Members of families living on different farms met in secret under cover of darkness. Music helped enslaved people hold on to their traditions, express their faith, and remain hopeful that freedom would come.

The approach of the American Revolution challenged everyone in Virginia to decide their loyalties. Arguments turned to action when the governor of Virginia, Lord Dunmore, ordered British marines to steal gunpowder from the Magazine. Dunmore claimed he had taken the powder to prevent a slave uprising, but Patriots believed he intended to keep local militia groups from fighting for independence.

The mayor of Williamsburg and other town leaders managed to keep an angry crowd from charging into the Palace, and eventually the governor did pay for the gunpowder. Still, Dunmore's action pushed many former Loyalists to embrace the Patriot cause. When two young men trying to break into the gunpowder Magazine were injured by a trap gun, the furious citizens who gathered could not be calmed. They stormed the building, and the militia mustered again. Soon Lord Dunmore fled with his family. As British rule in Virginia ended, war loomed on the horizon.

Read more of FELICITY'S stories,

available from booksellers and at *americangirl.com*

Classics

Felicity's classic series, now in two volumes:

Volume 1:
Love and Loyalty
When Felicity falls in love with a beautiful horse, she takes a great risk to save the mare from its cruel owner.

Volume 2:
A Stand for Independence
Felicity's friend Ben has run off to join the army. Now he needs her help—in secret. Should Felicity break Ben's trust?

Journey in Time

Travel back in time—and spend a day with Felicity!

Gunpowder and Tea Cakes
Experience the American Revolution with Felicity! Ride horses, visit the Governor's Palace—or get involved in a gunpowder plot! Choose your own path through this multiple-ending story.

Mysteries

More thrilling adventures with Felicity

Peril at King's Creek
Felicity is having a wonderful summer at her grandfather's plantation, until she discovers the farm—and her horse—are in danger!

Traitor in Williamsburg
Father has been accused of being a traitor! When he is arrested, Felicity must find out who is behind the terrible accusation.

Lady Margaret's Ghost
Felicity doesn't believe in ghosts . . . until odd and eerie things begin to happen once a mysterious package arrives.

A Sneak Peek at

Love and Loyalty

A Felicity Classic

Volume 1

What happens to Felicity?
Find out in the first volume of her classic stories.

r. Nye has a new horse, and I've a curiosity to see it," Felicity said as she and Ben made their way along the dusty main street of Williamsburg. She half expected Ben to tell her to run along home, but he didn't. *Sometimes I'm glad he's so quiet,* thought Felicity to herself.

Jiggy Nye's tannery was on the far edge of the town, where the pastures stretched off into the woods. Felicity could smell the tannery vats before she could see the tumbledown tannery shed. The vats were huge kettles full of yellow-brown ooze made of foul-smelling fish oil or sour beer. Mr. Nye soaked animal hides in them to make leather.

"Whoosh!" said Felicity. "The smell of the tannery is enough to make your hair curl!"

"Aye!" said Ben. "The whole business stinks."

Suddenly they heard angry shouts and a horse's frightened whinnies. "Down, ye hateful beast! Down, ye savage!" they heard Mr. Nye yell.

Felicity ran to the pasture gate. She saw Mr. Nye in the pasture, trying to back a horse between the shafts of a work cart. The horse was rearing up and whinnying. It jerked its head and pawed the air with its hooves. Mr. Nye was shouting and pulling on a rope that was tied around the horse's neck. "I'll beat ye down, I will," yelled Mr. Nye. "I'll beat ye!"

Ben caught up with Felicity and pulled her arm. "Stay back," he ordered.

"No! I want to see the horse," said Felicity. She stood behind the open gate and stared. The horse was wild-eyed and skinny. Its coat was rough and matted with dirt. Its mane and tail were knotted with burrs. But Felicity could see that it was a fine animal with long, strong legs and a proud, arched neck. "Oh, 'tis a beautiful horse," whispered Felicity. "Beautiful."

Mr. Nye and the horse both seemed to hear her at the same moment. The horse calmed and turned toward Felicity. That gave Mr. Nye a chance to tighten the rope around its neck. When the horse felt the rope, it went wild again. Mr. Nye was nearly pulled off the ground when it reared up on its hind legs.

"Ye beast!" Mr. Nye shouted. He glared at Ben and barked, "Help me! Get in here and grab this rope!"

Ben darted into the pen and grabbed the rope with Mr. Nye, but the horse reared and pawed the air more wildly than before.

"I'll beat the fire out of ye!" shouted Mr. Nye in a rage. He raised his whip to strike the horse.

"No!" cried Felicity. At that, the horse took off across the pasture, dragging Ben and Mr. Nye through the dust. They had to let go of the rope and give up.

Mr. Nye waved his arms and yelled at Felicity, "Get away with ye! You've spooked my horse, ye bothersome chit of a girl."

Felicity called out, "You spooked the horse yourself. You know you did!"

"Arrgh!" Mr. Nye snarled. He turned his red-rimmed eyes on Ben and growled, "What are ye doing here?"

"I've brought the bit and bridle you ordered from Master Merriman," Ben said.

Mr. Nye held out his hand. "Give it here."

Ben stepped back. "I'm to wait for payment."

"Get away with ye!" shouted Mr. Nye. "Keep your blasted bit. That horse won't take the bit no matter. Go now, before I take my whip to the two of ye. Hear me?"

Ben turned to go, but Felicity backed away slowly. She couldn't stop watching the beautiful horse.

It was running back and forth across the pasture, trapped inside the fence.

"Felicity, come along!" said Ben.

Felicity turned and followed Ben, but she did not even see the road in front of her. "Isn't she beautiful, Ben?" Felicity said. "Isn't she a dream of a horse?"

"Aye," agreed Ben. "She's a chestnut mare, a blood horse."

"That means she's a thoroughbred, doesn't it?" said Felicity.

"Aye. It means she was trained to be a gentleman's mount," said Ben. "That horse is not bred to drag a work cart."

"She was never meant to belong to the likes of Mr. Nye!" Felicity exclaimed. "She's much too fine! Oh, just once I'd love to ride a horse like that!"

"She'd be too fast for you," said Ben. "You'd never stay on her." He shook his head grimly. "Besides, that horse won't trust anyone after the way Mr. Nye is treating her. She won't let anyone on her back ever again. That horse has gone vicious."

Felicity heard what Ben said, but she didn't believe it. She'd seen the look of frantic anger in the

horse's eyes. But Felicity had seen something else, too. Under the wildness there was spirit, not viciousness. Just as under the mud and burrs there was a beautiful reddish-gold coat, as bright as a new copper penny. "Penny," whispered Felicity.

"What?" asked Ben.

"Penny," said Felicity. "That's what I'm going to call that horse. She's the color of a new copper penny. It's a good name for her, isn't it?"

"Aye," said Ben. "Because she's an independent-minded horse, that's for certain. Call her Penny for her inde*pen*dence, too."

Felicity smiled. From then on, she thought of the horse as Penny—beautiful, independent, bright, shining Penny.

By the time Felicity and Ben walked to the middle of town, the sun was melting on the horizon. They hurried along to the Merrimans' house.

"Felicity Merriman!" exclaimed her mother. "Wherever have you been all this time?"

"Ben and I went out to the tannery," said Felicity. "And, oh, Mother! We saw the most beautiful horse!"

"A horse?" asked Mrs. Merriman.

"It's Jiggy Nye's new horse, I wager," said Mr. Merriman.

Ben handed him the harness and bit. "Mr. Nye didn't buy these things, sir. He can't control the horse enough to harness it. 'Tis a headstrong, independent-minded horse, a bright chestnut mare, and fast as fire."

"How did Jiggy Nye come to have such a horse?" asked Mrs. Merriman.

"No one knows for sure," said Ben. "Mr. Nye says he won the horse in a bet from a man who found it straying in the woods. He says the man put a notice in the newspaper. The notice said that whoever lost the horse should come to claim it, but no one ever came. That's just Mr. Nye's story, though. It's hard to trust his word."

Felicity had never heard Ben talk so much. She was surprised at all he knew.

"It's a pity Jiggy's got hold of the horse," said Mr. Merriman. He shook his head. "It will not end well, I fear."

Felicity could tell by the look on her father's face that Penny was in danger. She made up her mind to go back to the tannery and see Penny as soon as she could.

About the Author

KATHLEEN ERNST grew up in Baltimore, Maryland—not too far from Williamsburg, Virginia, where Felicity's stories are set. Ms. Ernst loved visiting Colonial Williamsburg with her family as a child, and she has returned many times over the years, most recently to research this story about Felicity. She lives in Wisconsin with her husband and cat, where she writes award-winning mysteries for children and adults.